Putuguq & Kublu
AND THE QALUPALIK!

INHABIT
MEDIA

Iqaluit • Toronto

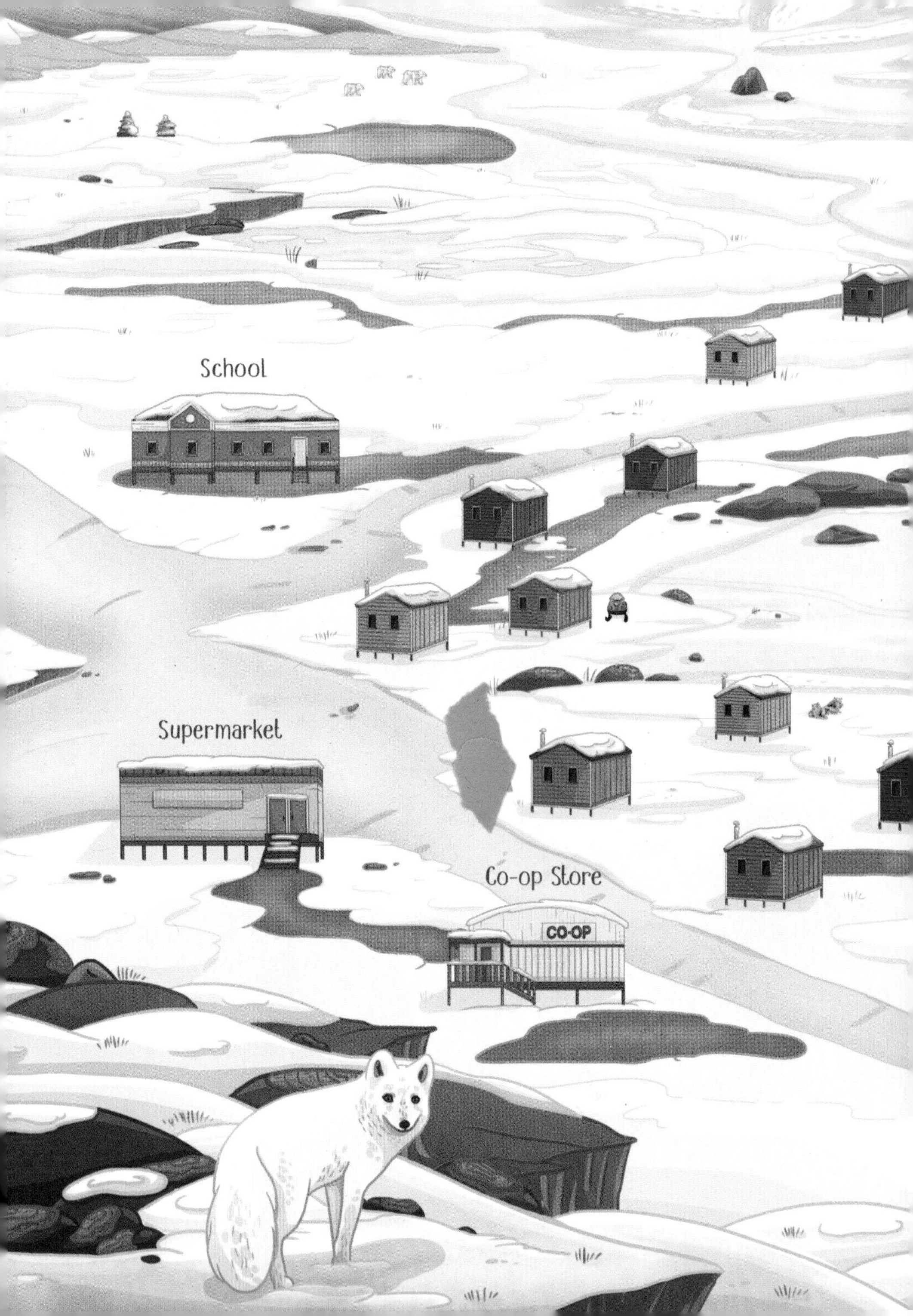
School
Supermarket
Co-op Store
CO-OP

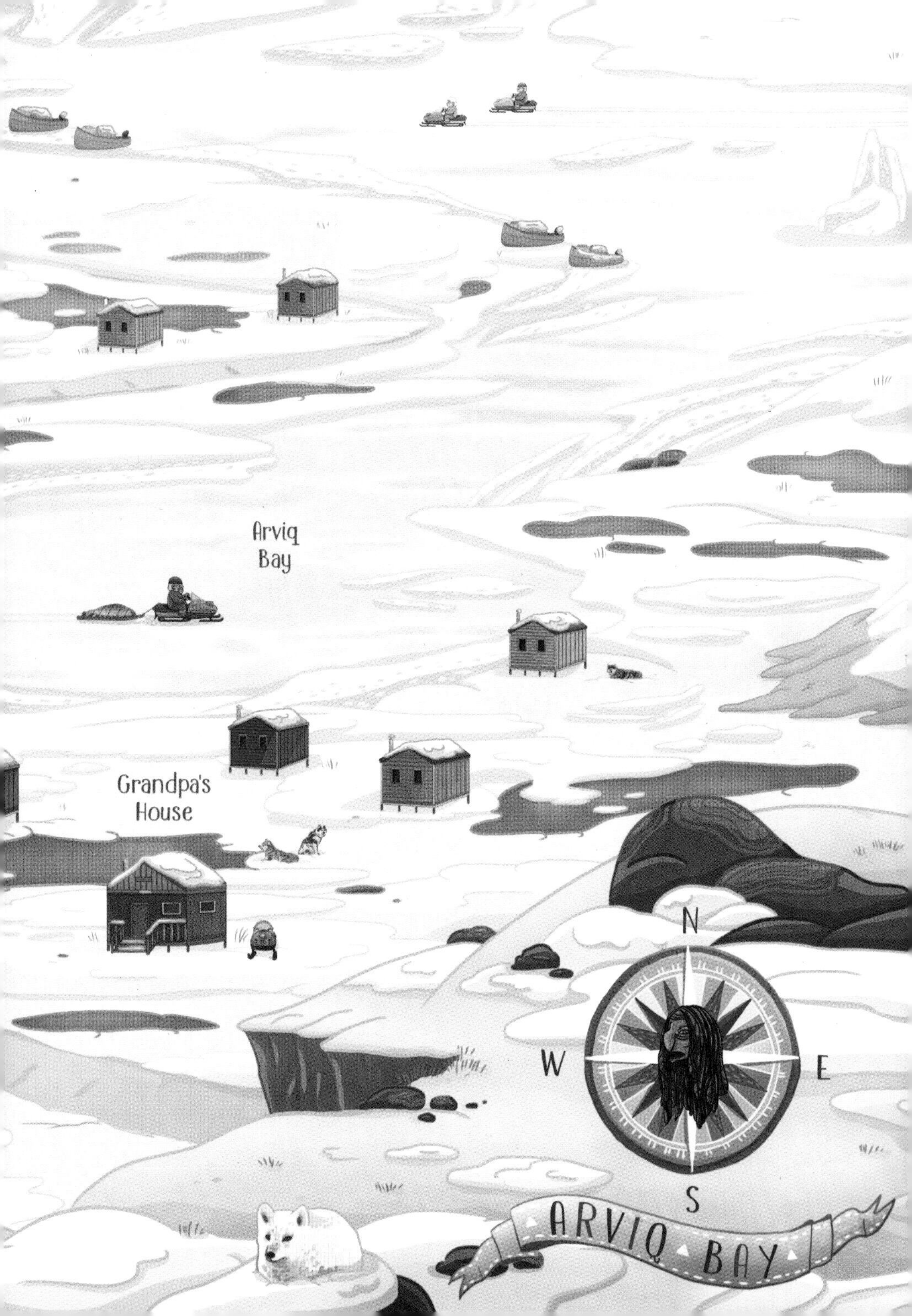
Arviq
Bay
Grandpa's
House
N
W
E
S
ARVIQ BAY

Published by Inhabit Media Inc. | www.inhabitmedia.com

Inhabit Media Inc. (Iqaluit) P.O. Box 11125, Iqaluit, Nunavut, XOA 1HO
(Toronto) 191 Eglinton Ave. East, Suite 310, Toronto, Ontario, M4P 1K1

Design and layout copyright © 2018 Inhabit Media Inc.
Text copyright © 2018 Danny Christopher
Illustrations by Astrid Arijanto copyright © 2018 Inhabit Media Inc.

Editors: Neil Christopher and Kelly Ward
Art director: Danny Christopher
Designer: Astrid Arijanto

We acknowledge the support of the Canada Council for the Arts for our
publishing program.

This project was made possible in part by the Government of Canada.

ISBN: 978-1-77227-228-4

Printed in Canada.

Library and Archives Canada Cataloguing in Publication

Akulukjuk, Roselynn, author
Putuguq & Kublu and the Qalupalik! / by Roselynn Akulukjuk
and Danny Christopher ; illustrated by Astrid Arijanto.

ISBN 978-1-77227-228-4 (softcover)

1. Comics (Graphic works). I. Christopher, Danny, author II. Arijanto,
Astrid, illustrator III. Title. IV. Title: Putuguq and Kublu and the Qalupalik!

PN6733.A37P88 2018   j741.5'971   C2018-904675-9

By Roselynn Akulukjuk and Danny Christopher
Illustrated by Astrid Arijanto

Putuguq & Kublu

AND THE QALUPALIK!

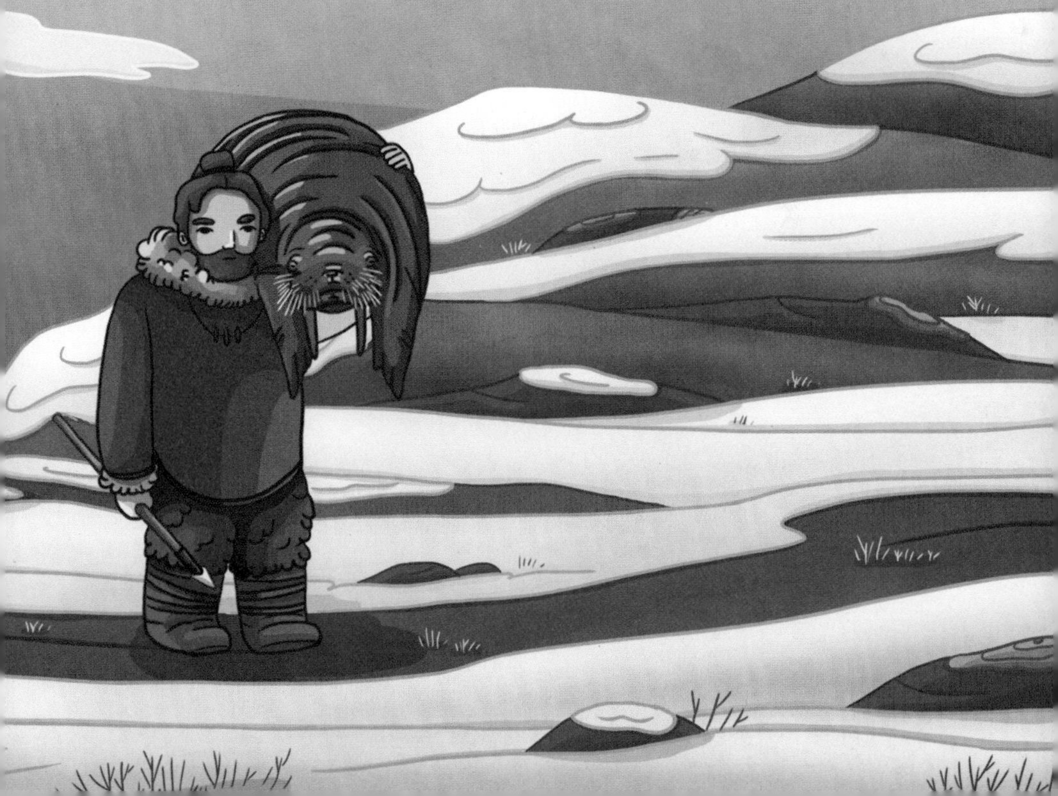

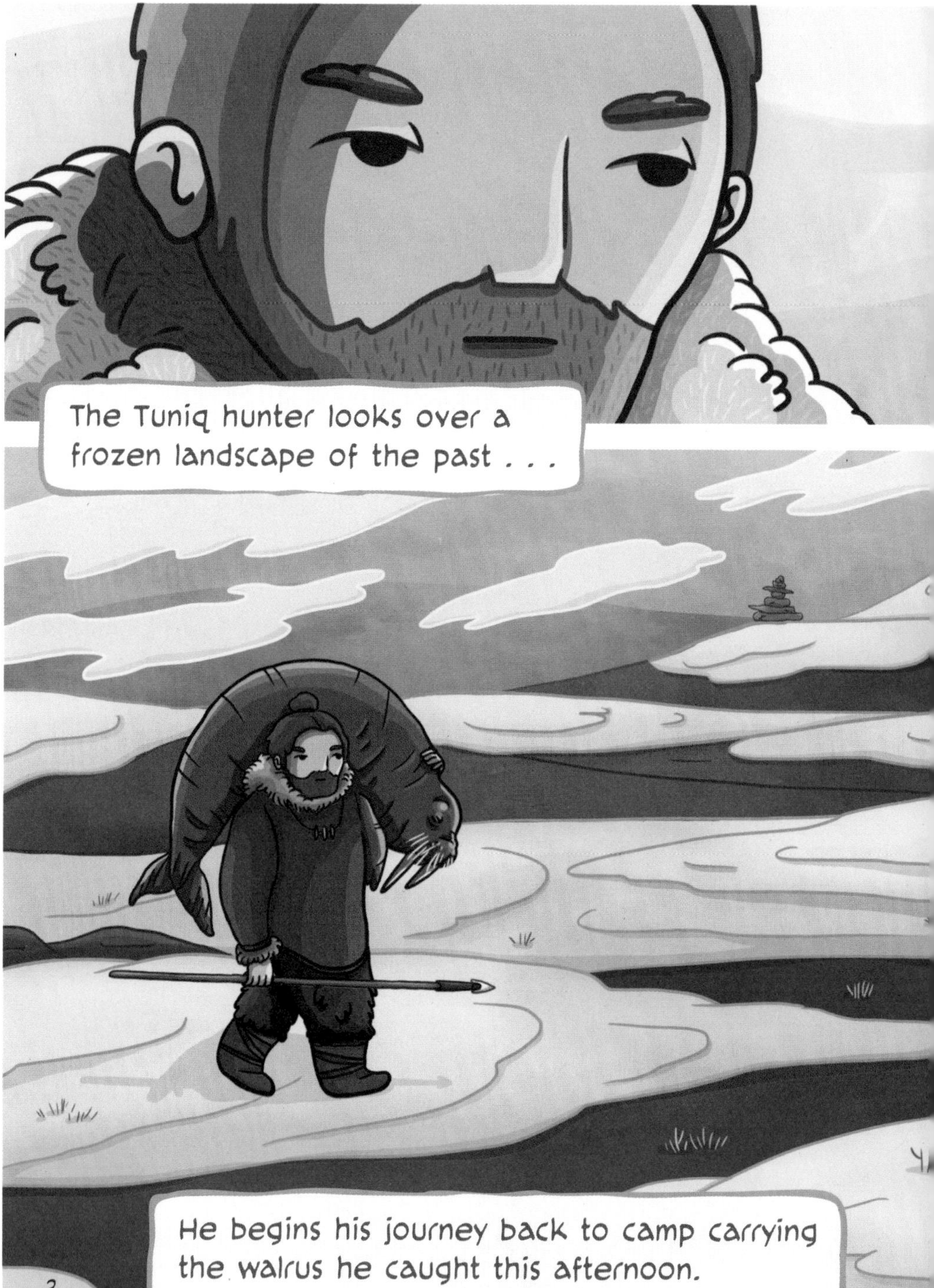
The Tuniq hunter looks over a frozen landscape of the past . . .
He begins his journey back to camp carrying the walrus he caught this afternoon.

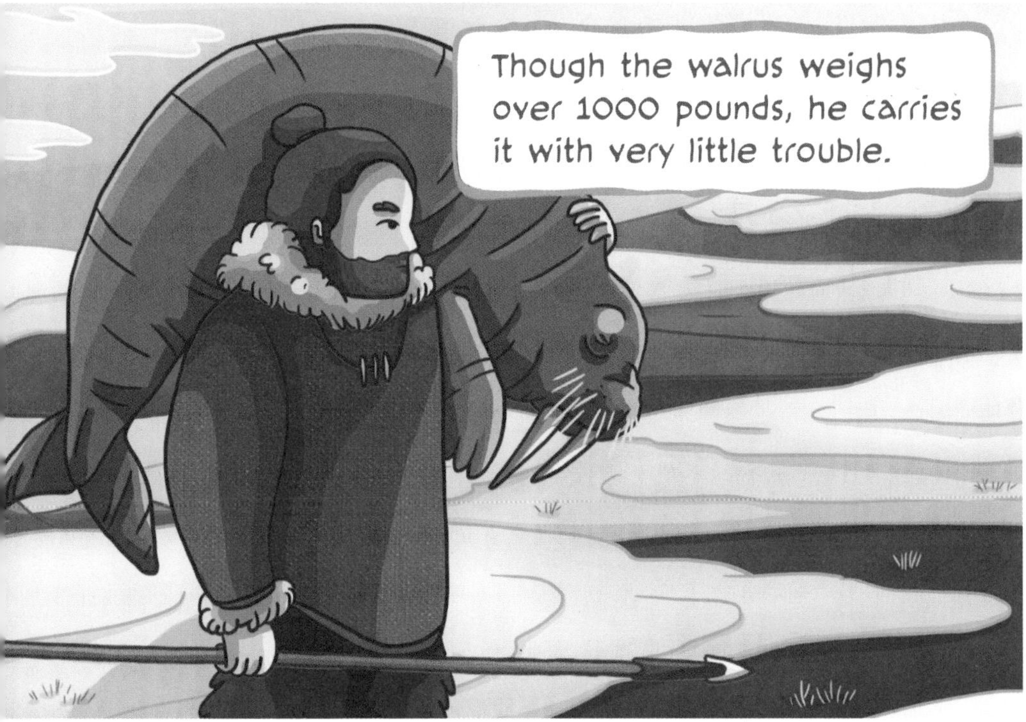
Though the walrus weighs over 1000 pounds, he carries it with very little trouble.

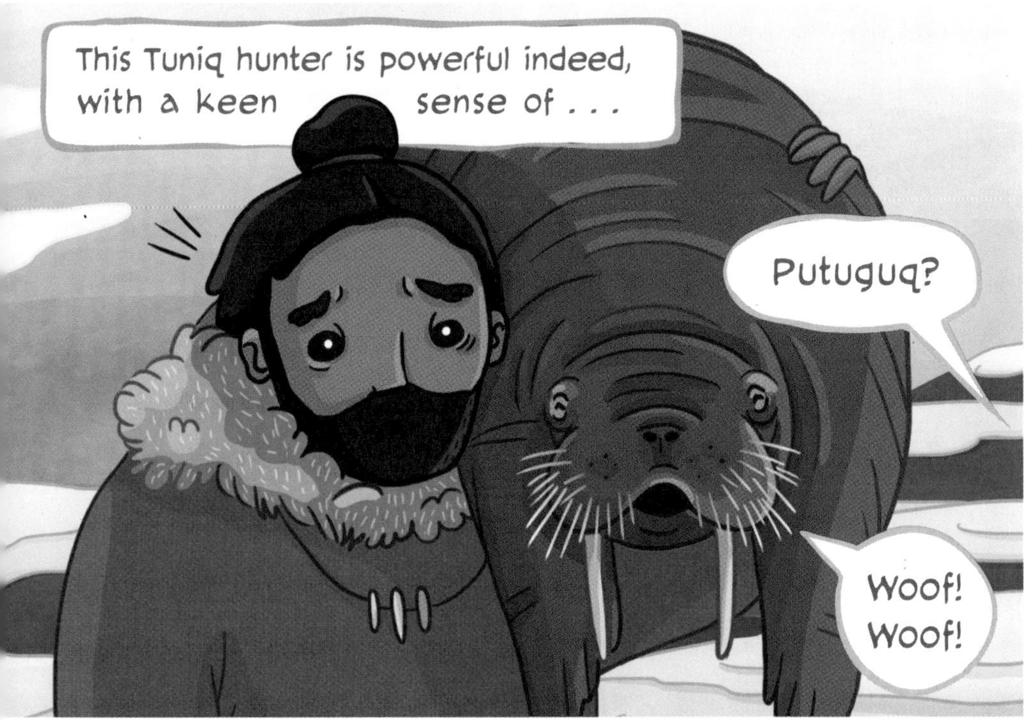
This Tuniq hunter is powerful indeed, with a keen sense of . . .
Putuguq?
Woof! Woof!

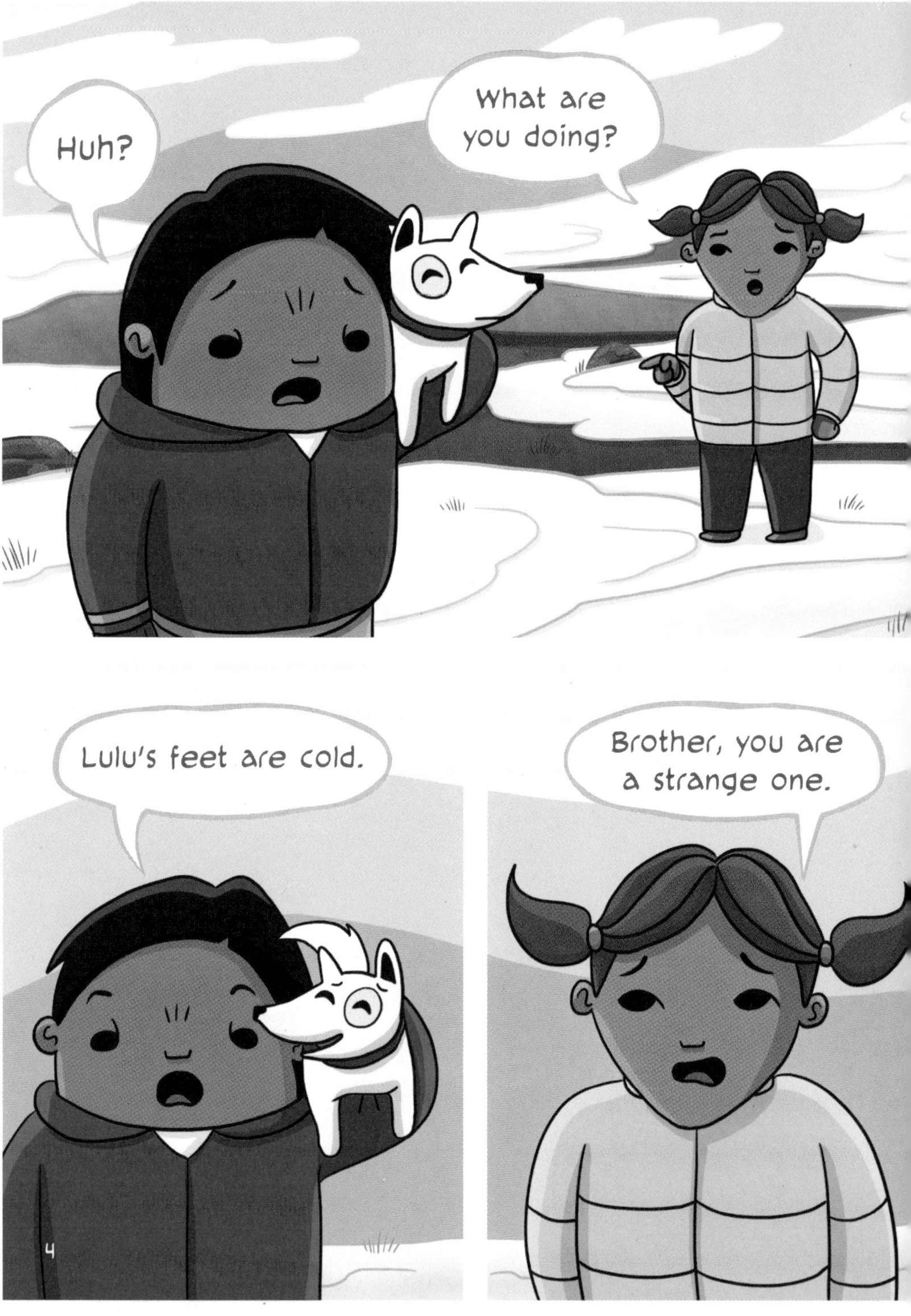
Huh?
What are you doing?
Lulu's feet are cold.
Brother, you are a strange one.

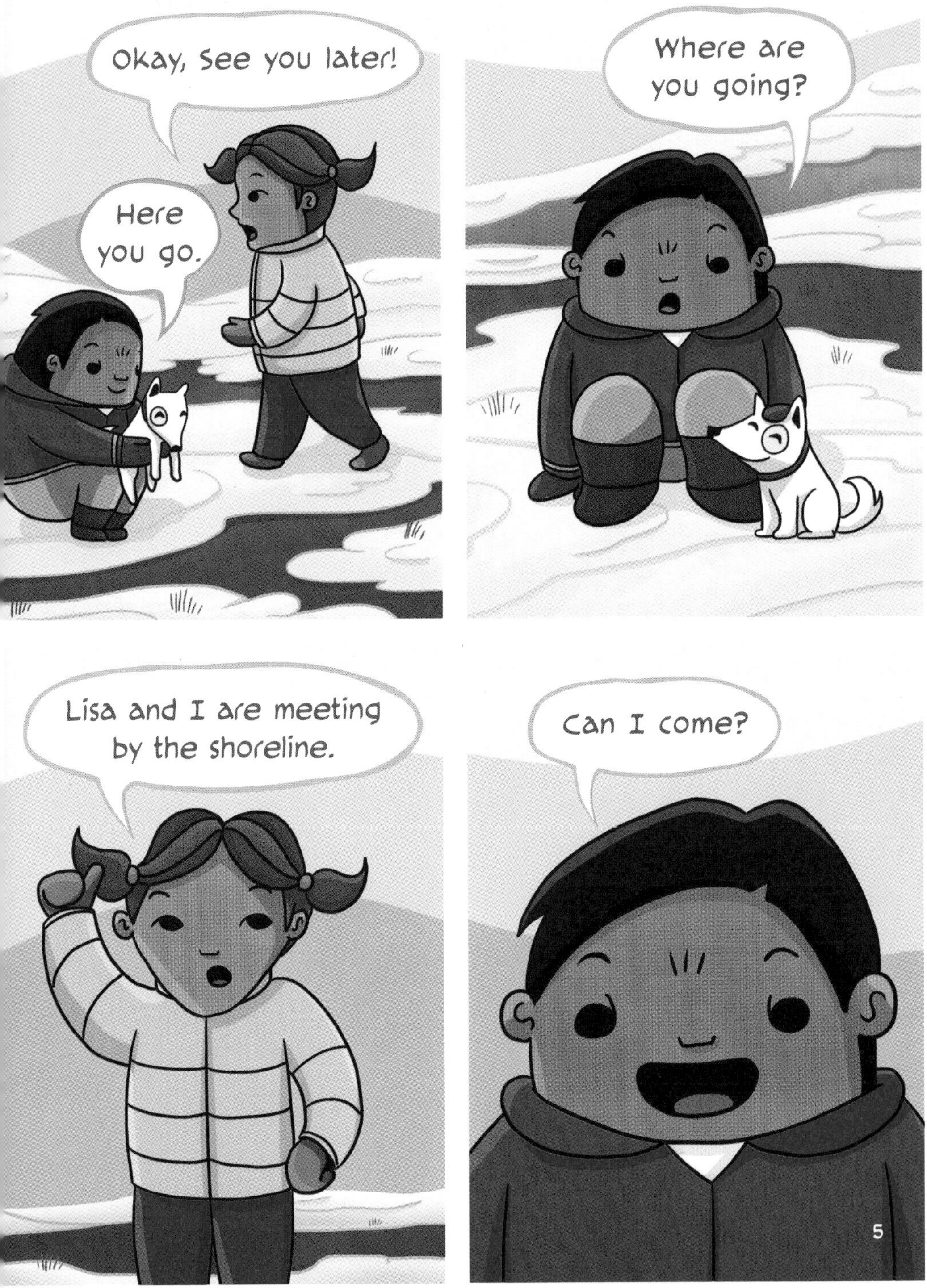
Okay, see you later!
Here you go.
Where are you going?
Lisa and I are meeting by the shoreline.
Can I come?

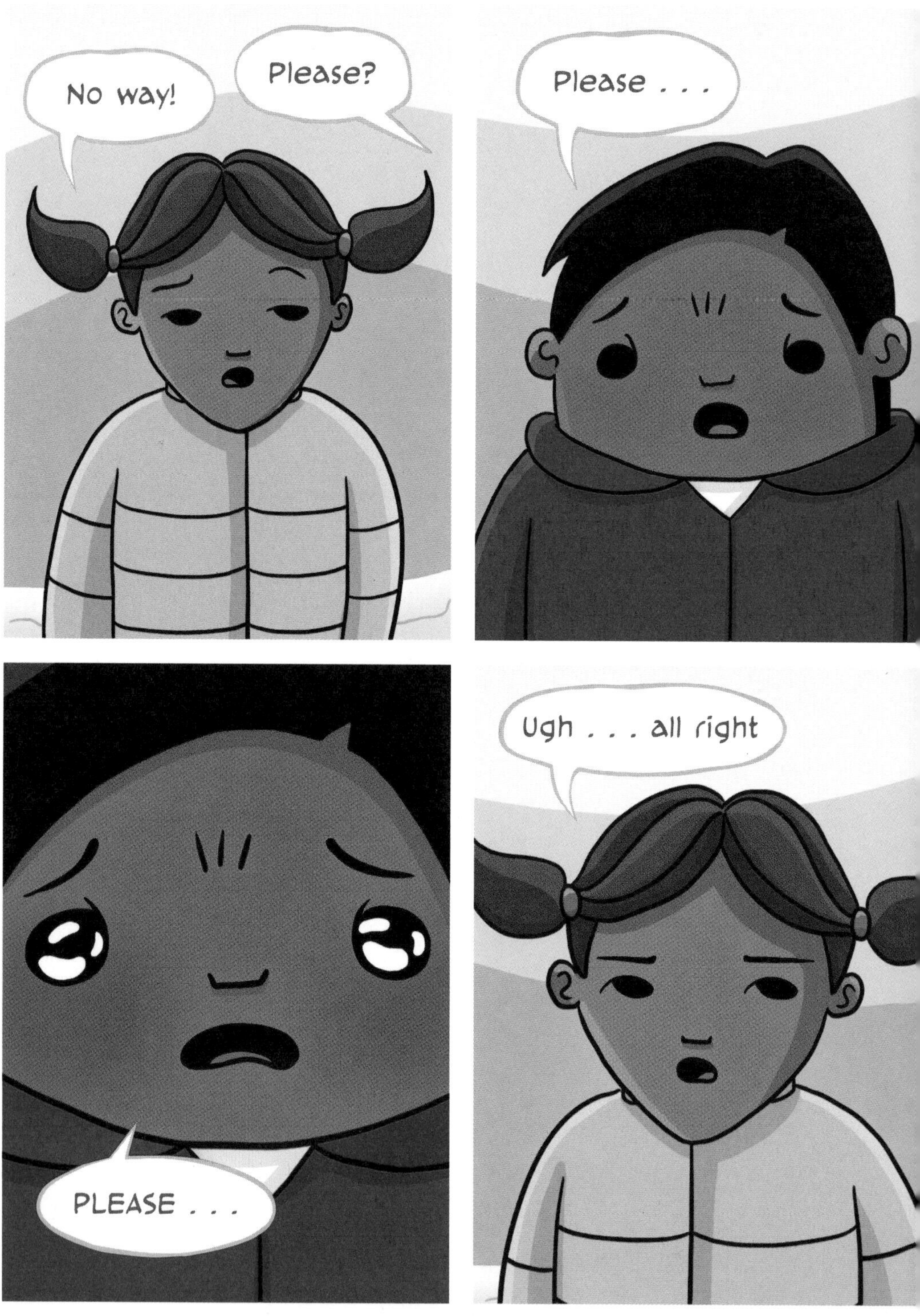
No way!
Please?
Please . . .
PLEASE . . .
Ugh . . . all right

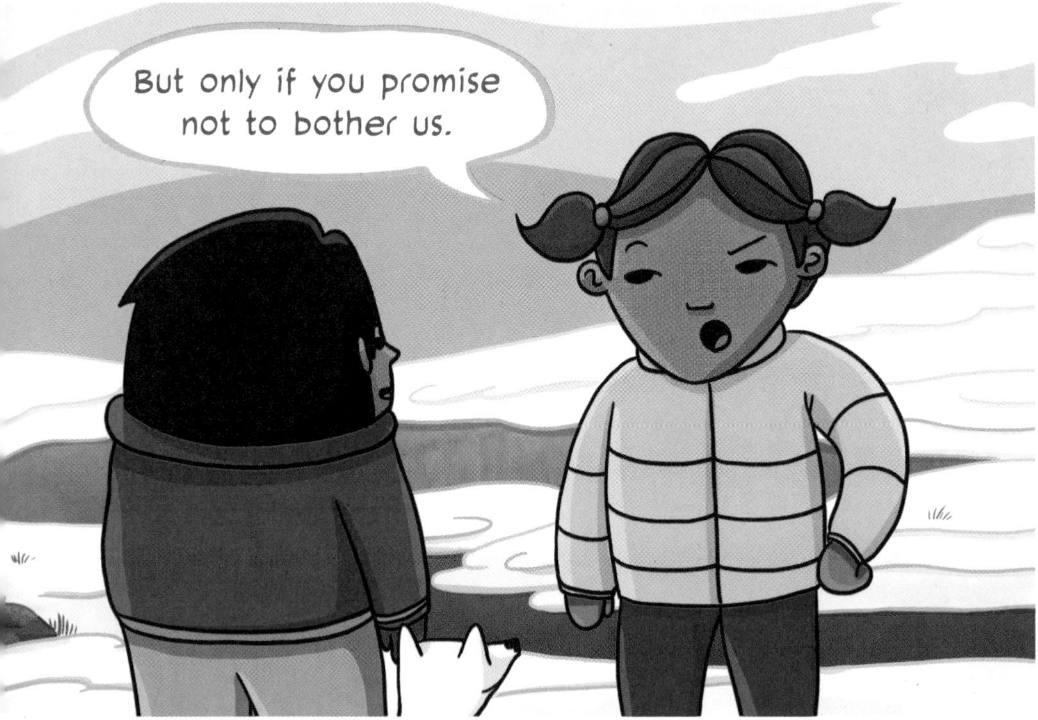
But only if you promise not to bother us.

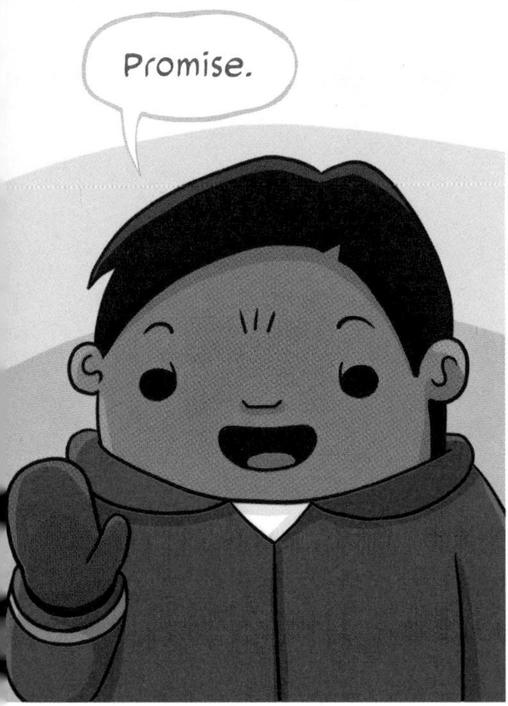
Promise.

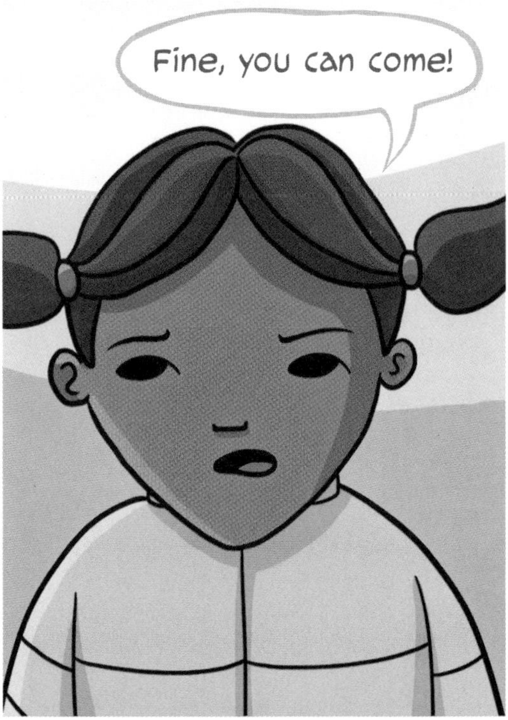
Fine, you can come!

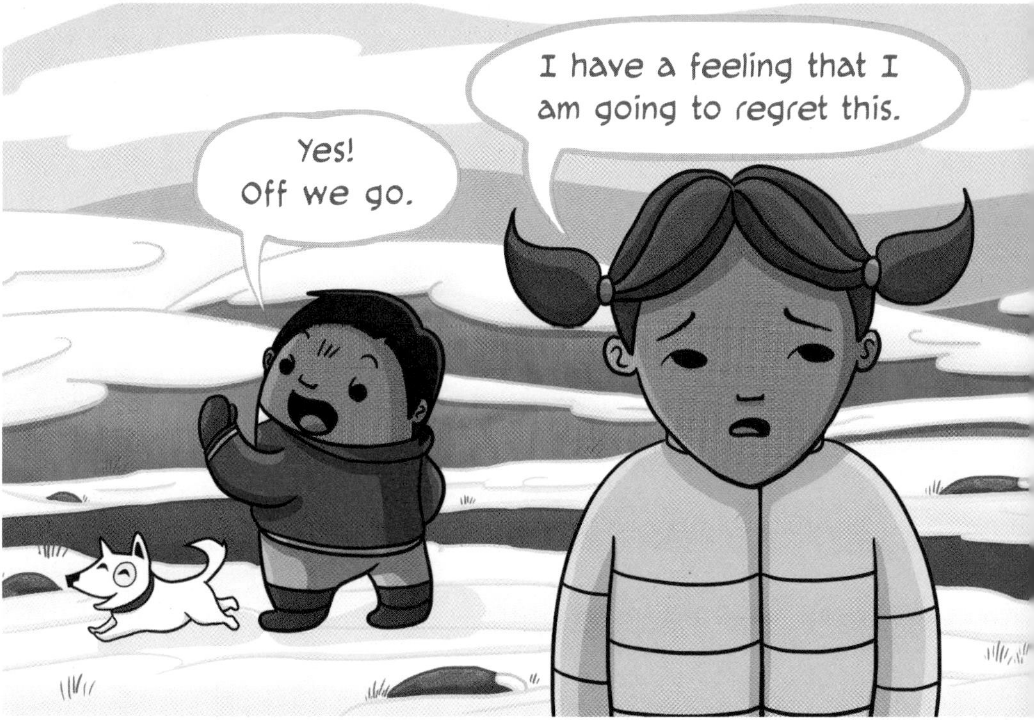
Yes!
Off we go.
I have a feeling that I am going to regret this.

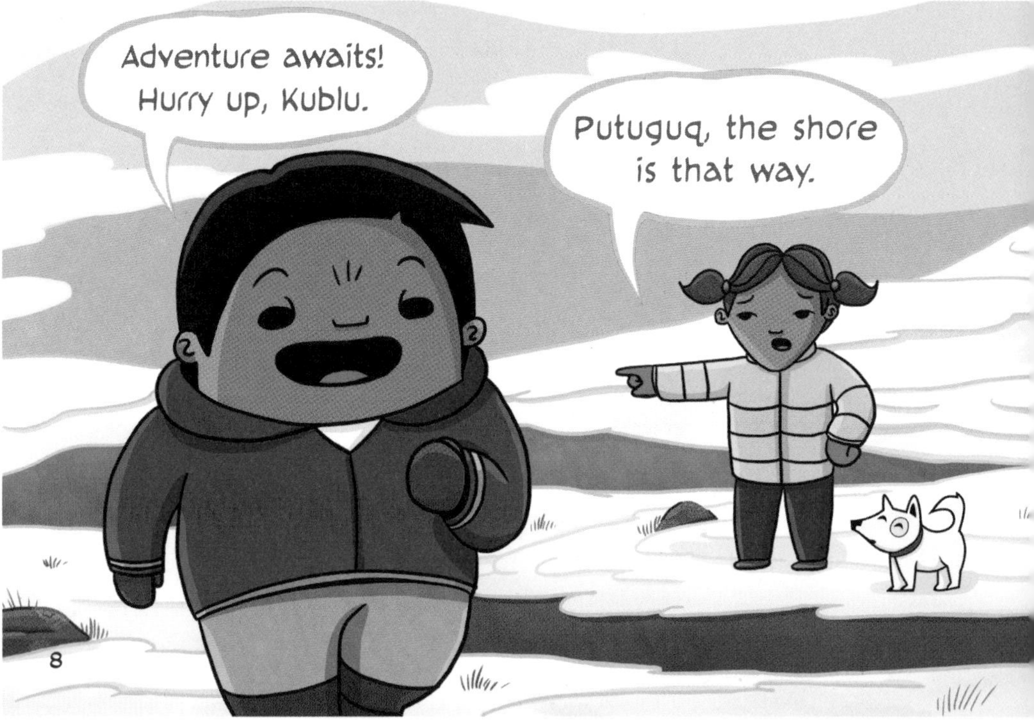
Adventure awaits! Hurry up, Kublu.
Putuguq, the shore is that way.

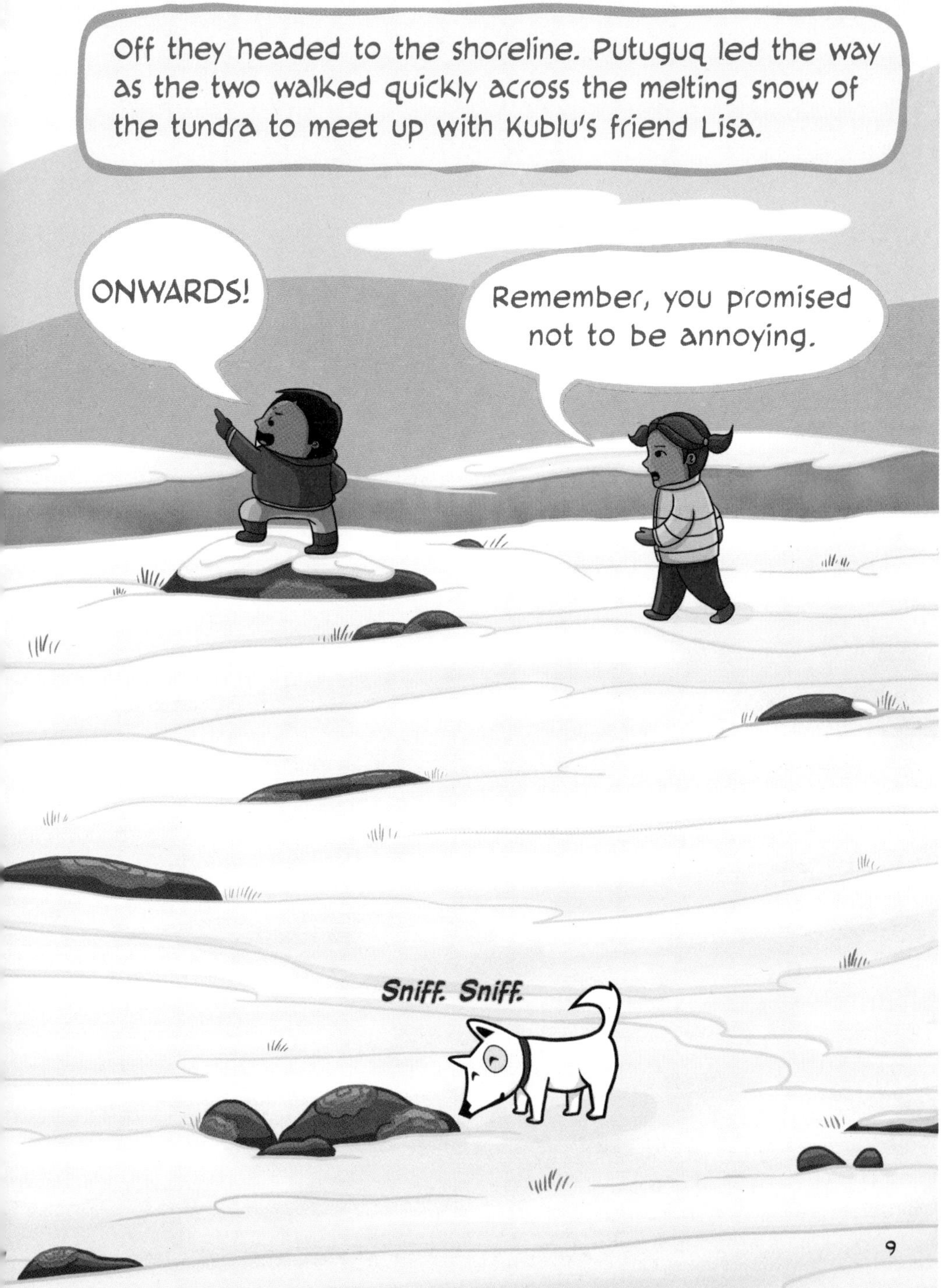
Off they headed to the shoreline. Putuguq led the way as the two walked quickly across the melting snow of the tundra to meet up with Kublu's friend Lisa.
ONWARDS!
Remember, you promised not to be annoying.
Sniff. Sniff.

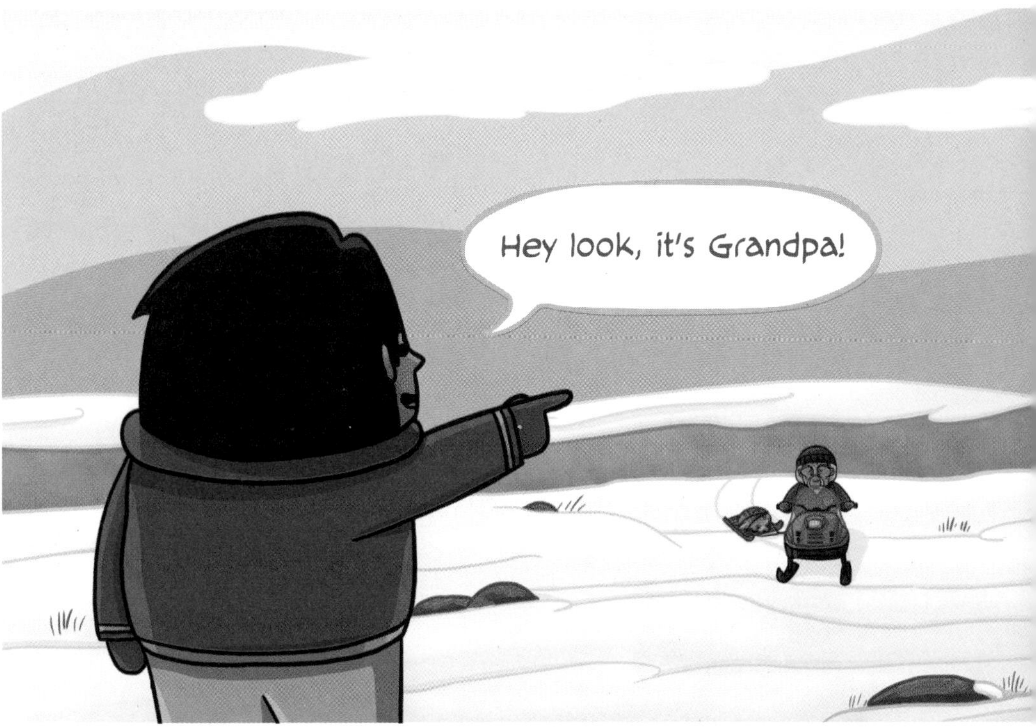
Hey look, it's Grandpa!

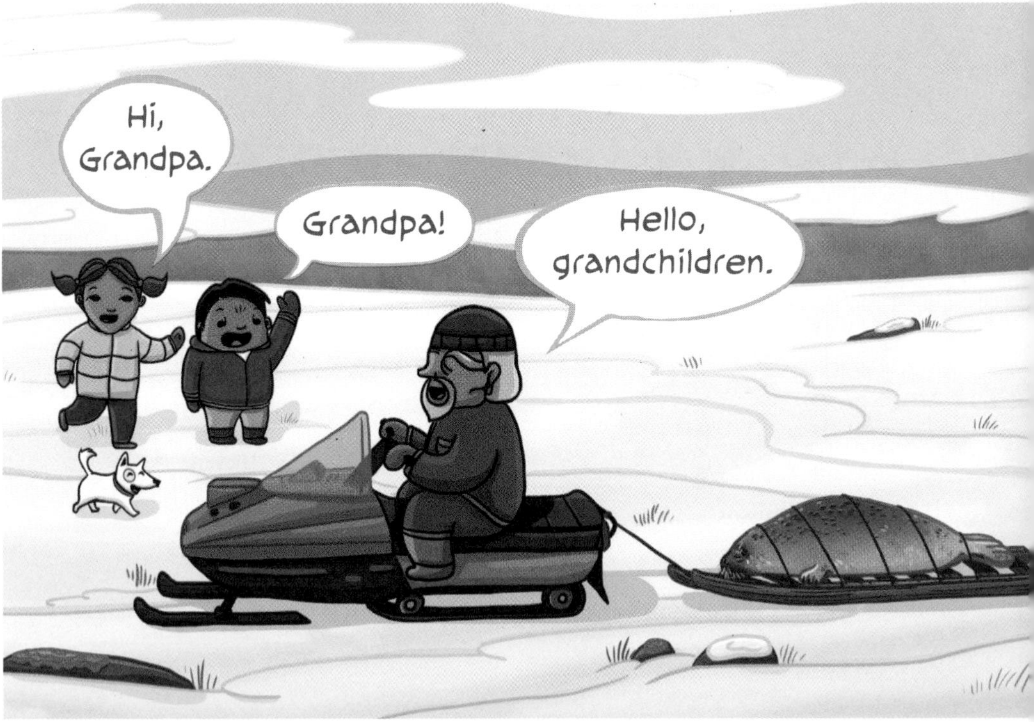
Hi,
Grandpa.
Grandpa!
Hello,
grandchildren.

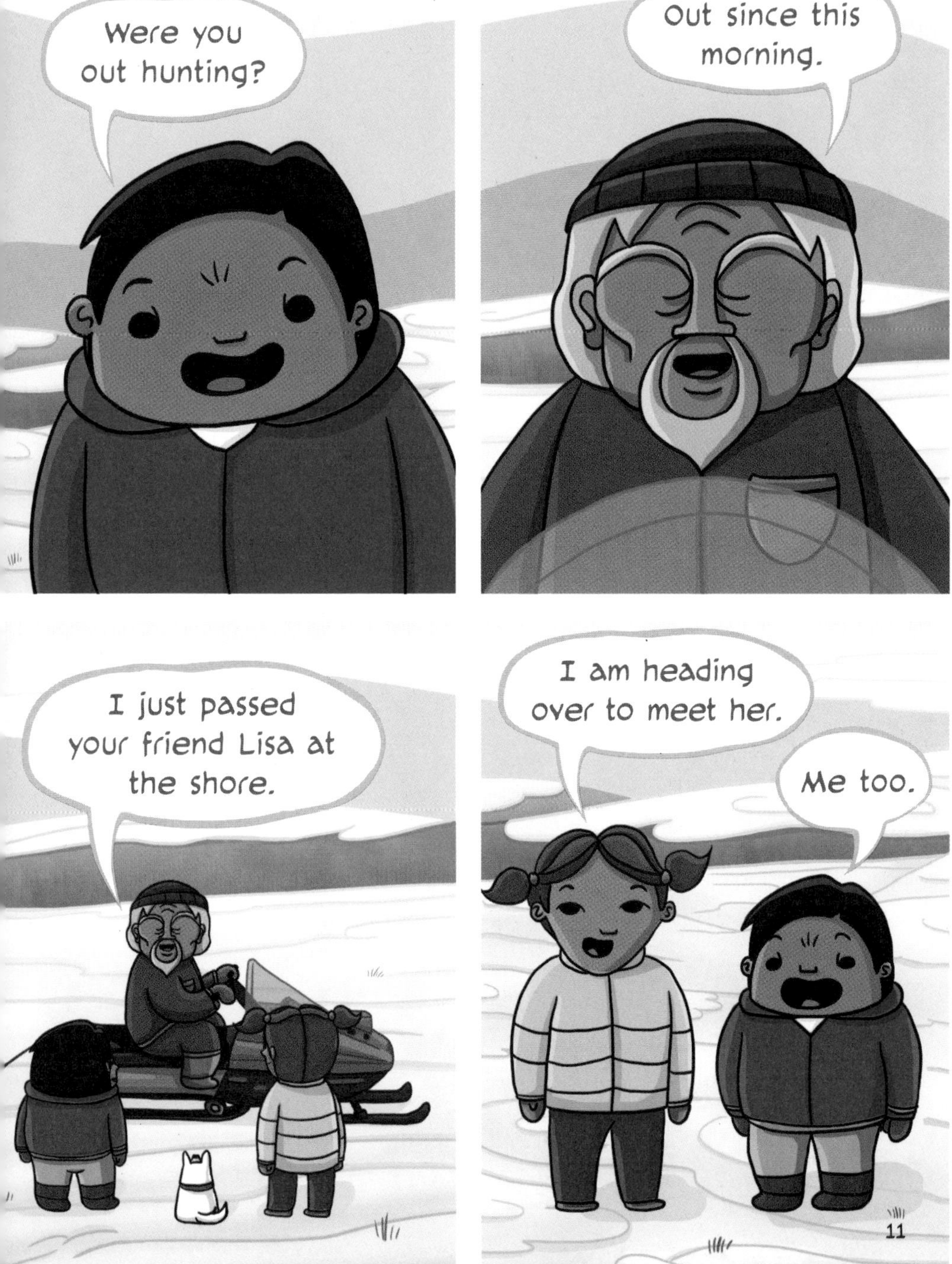
Were you out hunting?
Out since this morning.
I just passed your friend Lisa at the shore.
I am heading over to meet her.
Me too.

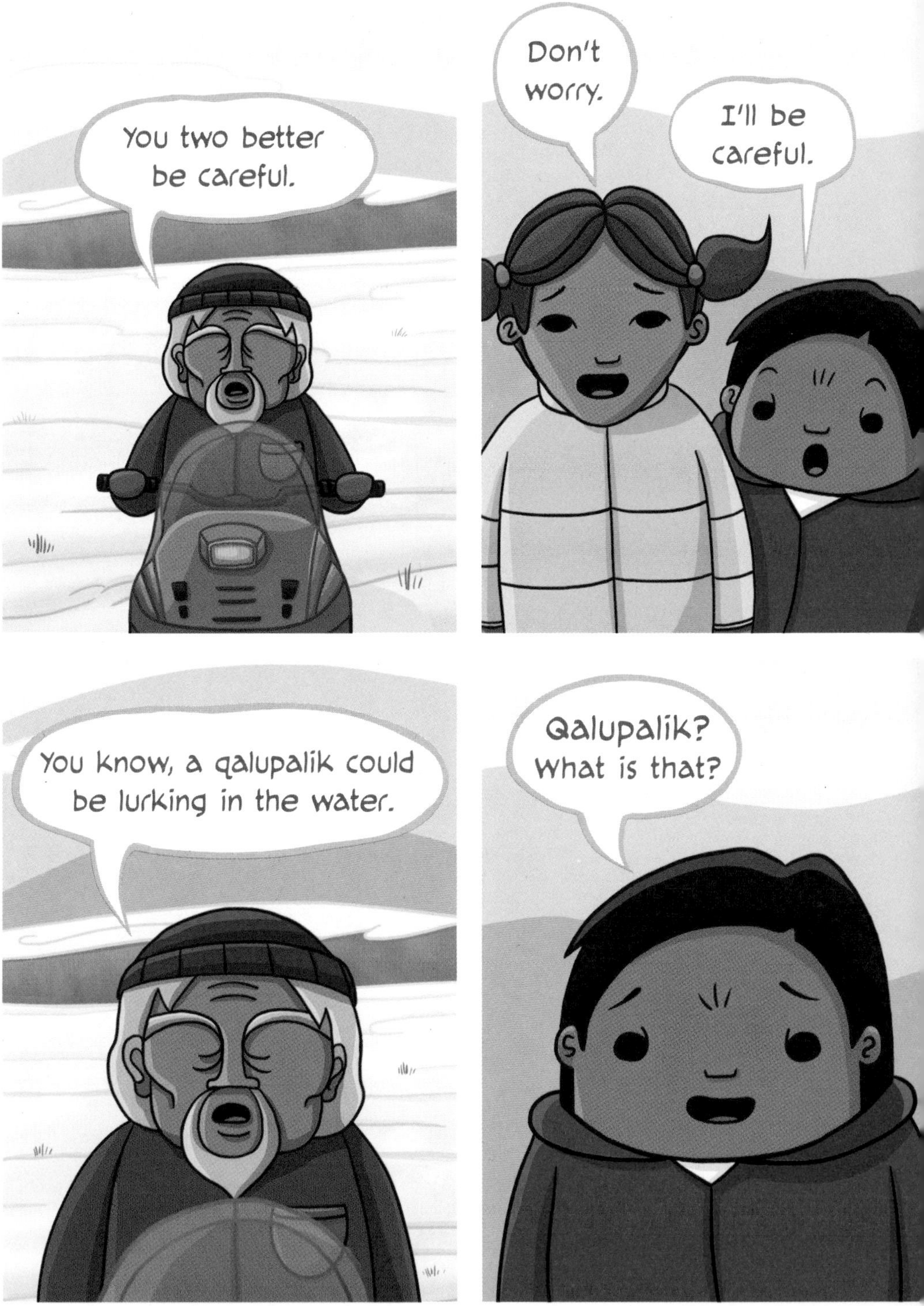
You two better be careful.
Don't worry.
I'll be careful.
You know, a qalupalik could be lurking in the water.
Qalupalik? What is that?

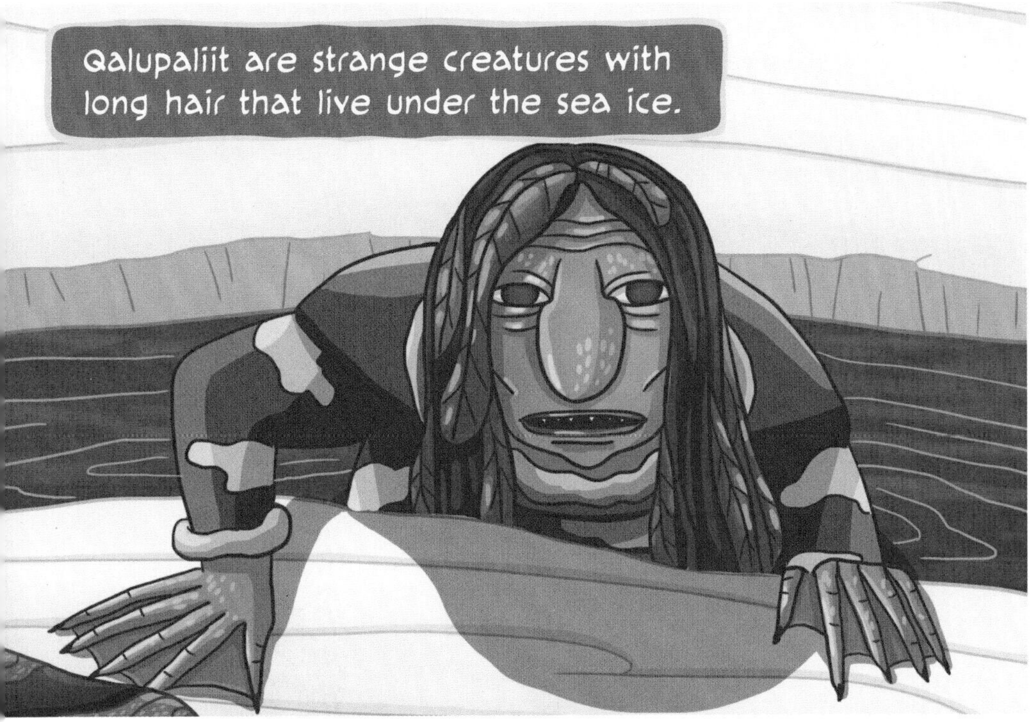
Qalupaliit are strange creatures with long hair that live under the sea ice.

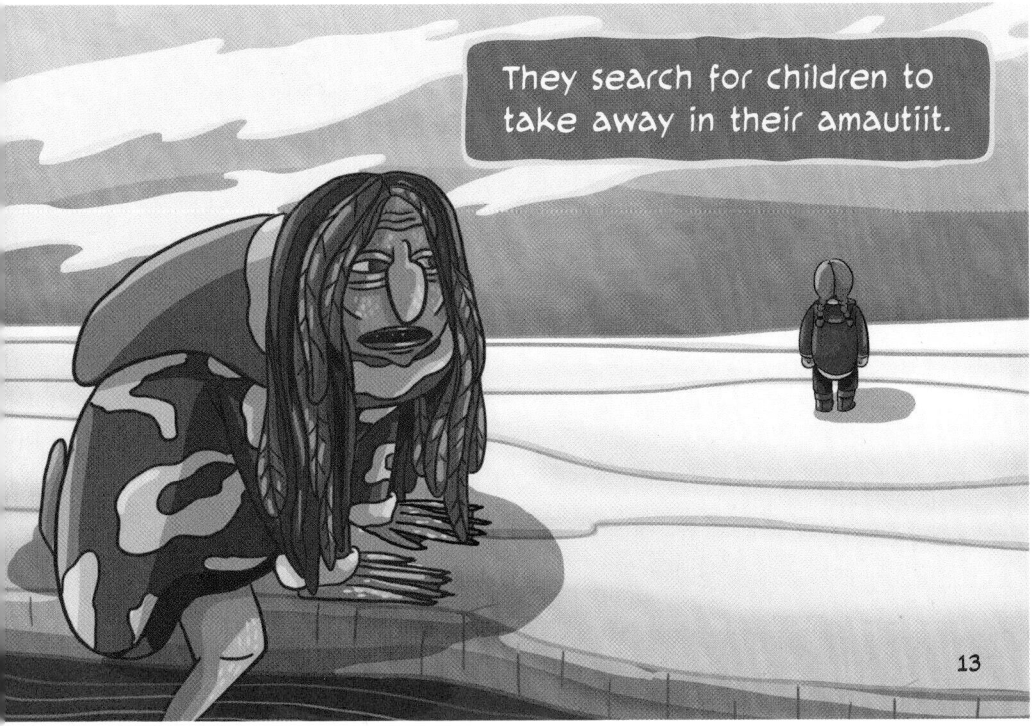
They search for children to take away in their amautiit.

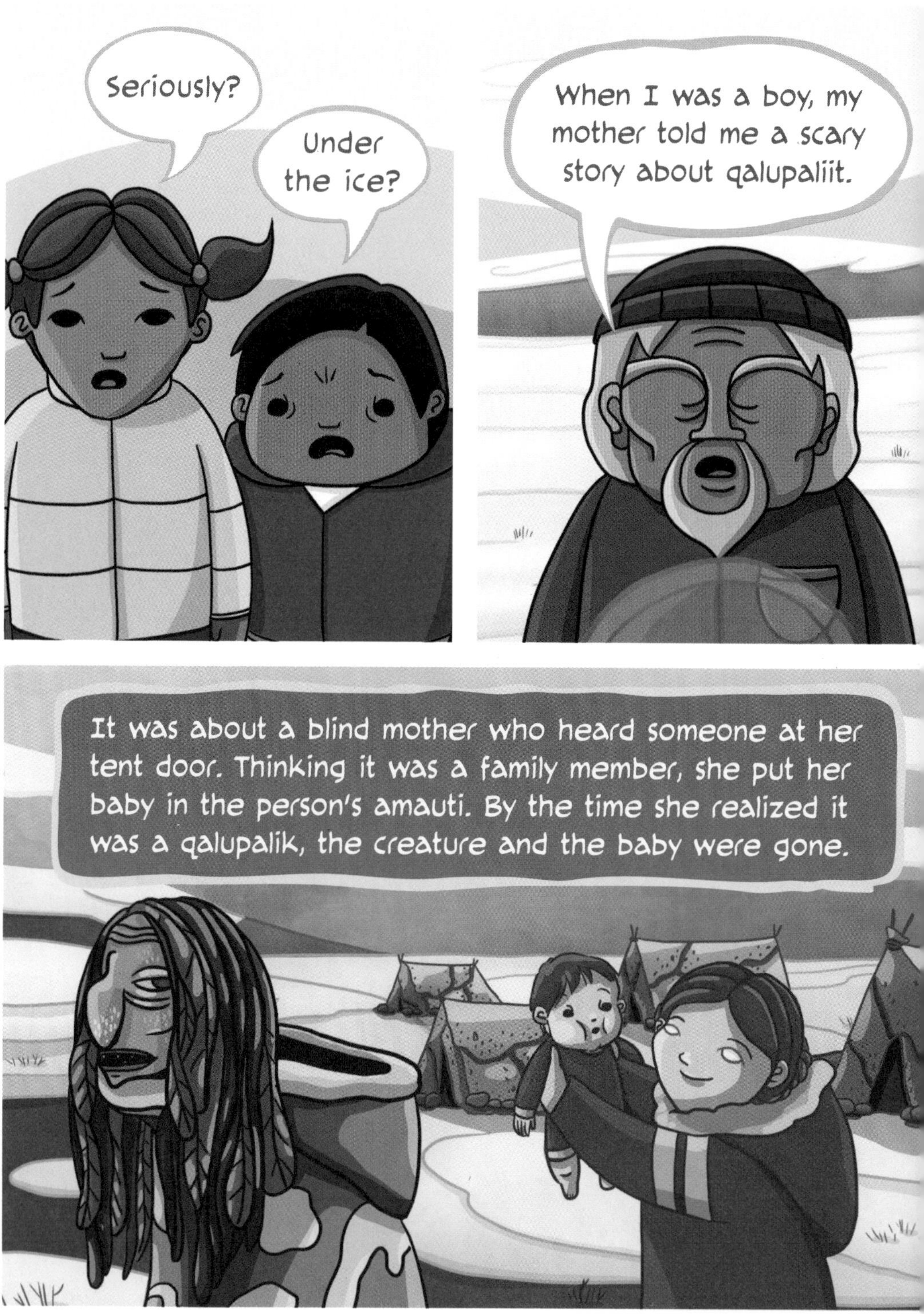
Seriously?
Under the ice?
When I was a boy, my mother told me a scary story about qalupaliit.
It was about a blind mother who heard someone at her tent door. Thinking it was a family member, she put her baby in the person's amauti. By the time she realized it was a qalupalik, the creature and the baby were gone.

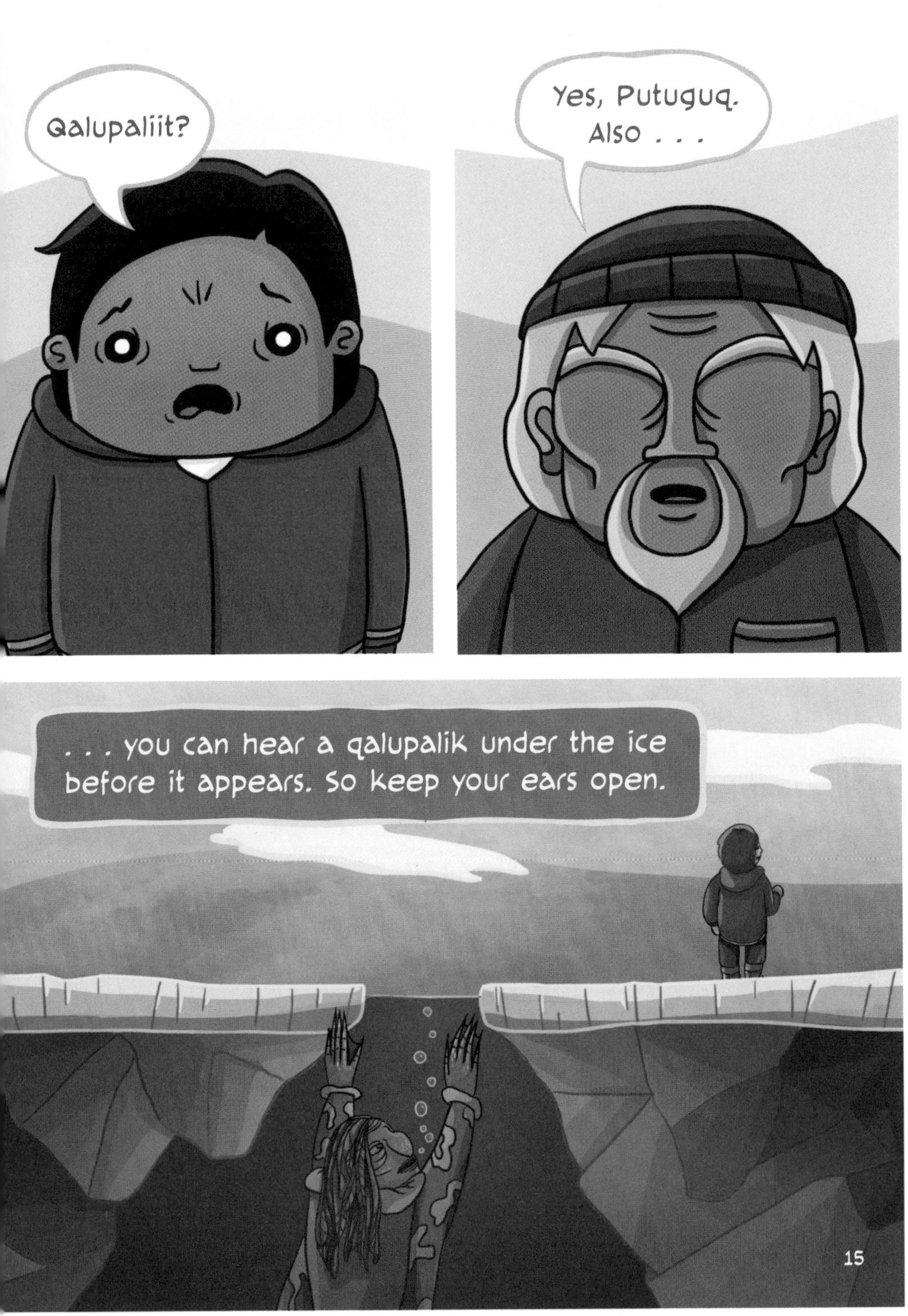
Qalupaliit?
Yes, Putuguq. Also . . .
. . . you can hear a qalupalik under the ice before it appears. So keep your ears open.

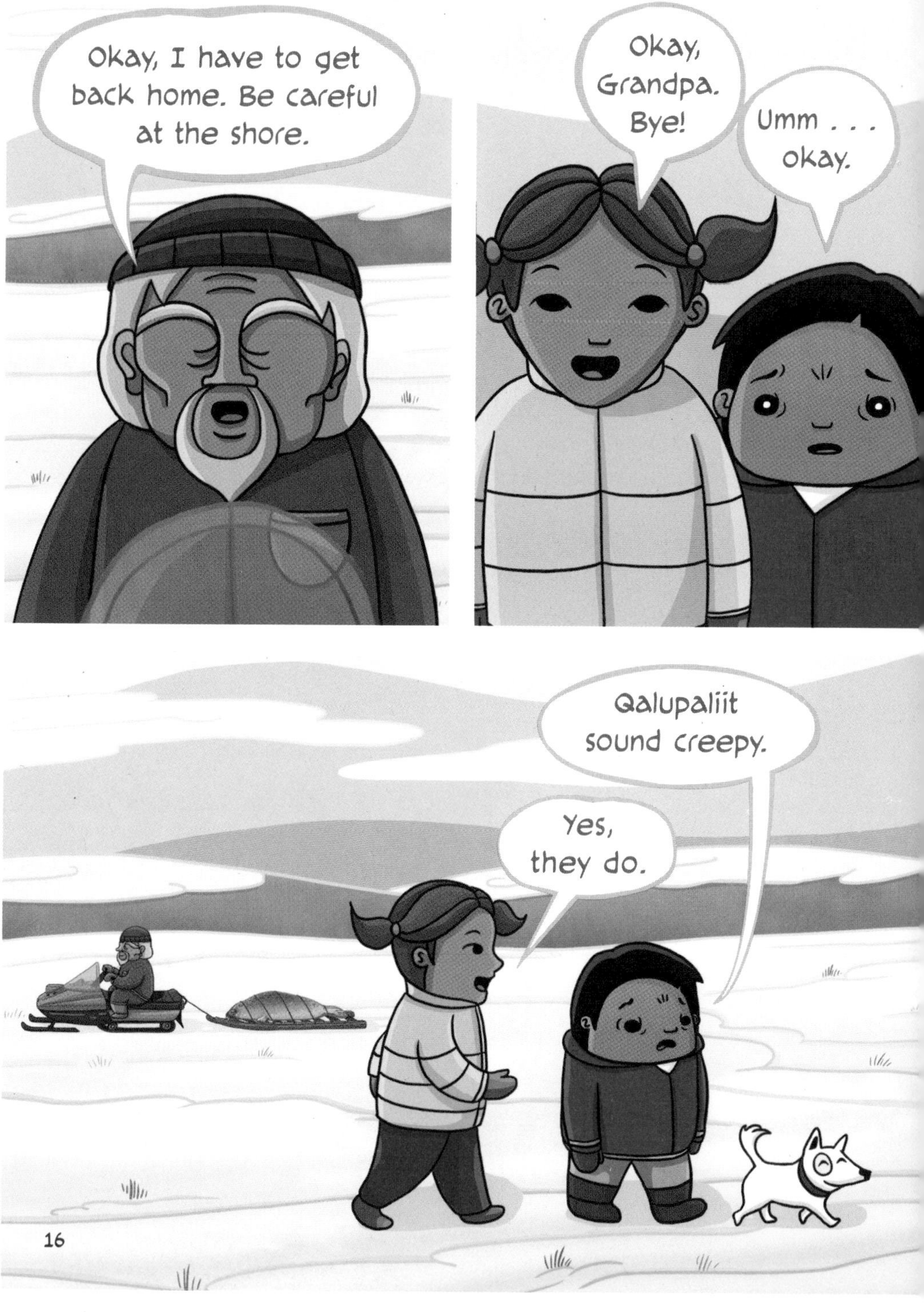
Okay, I have to get back home. Be careful at the shore.
Okay, Grandpa. Bye!
Umm . . . okay.
Qalupaliit sound creepy.
Yes, they do.

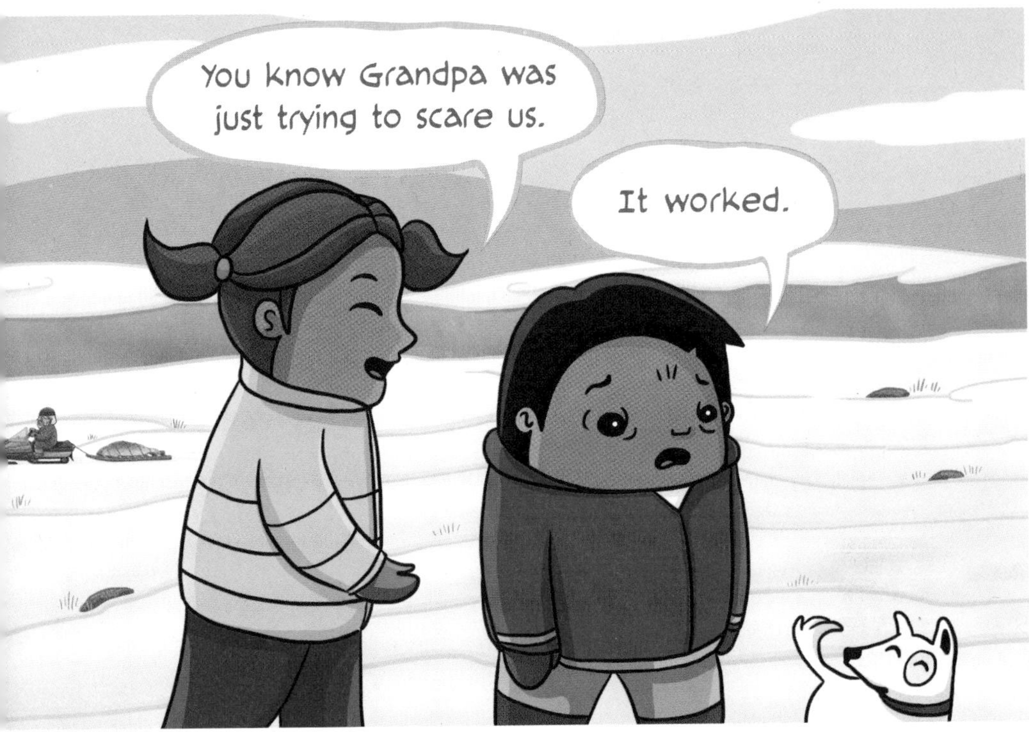
You know Grandpa was just trying to scare us.
It worked.

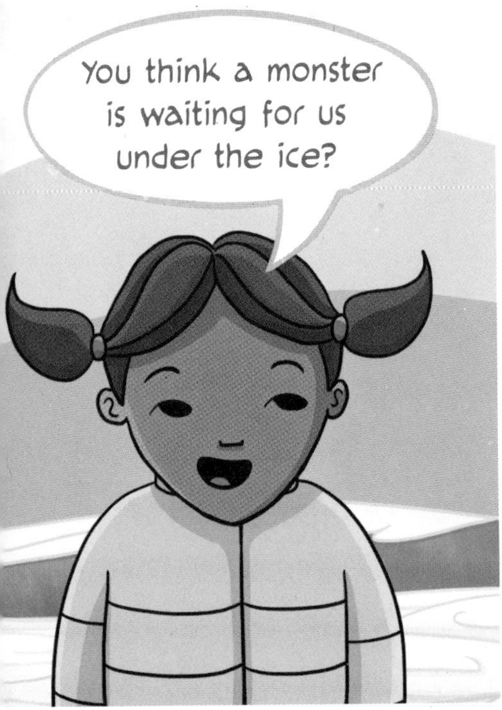
You think a monster is waiting for us under the ice?

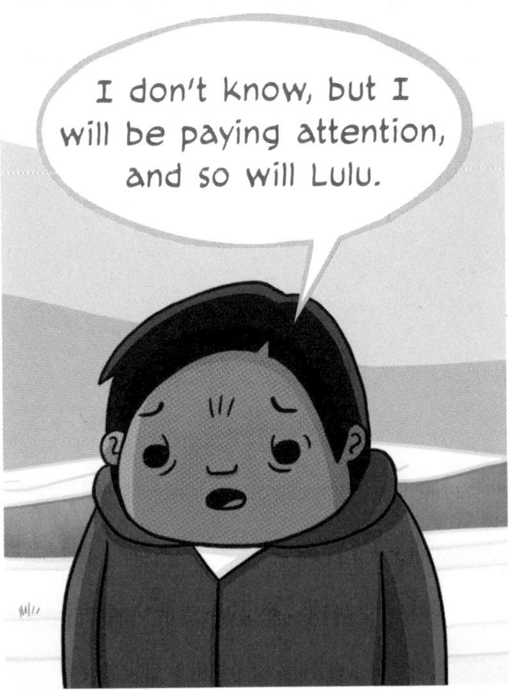
I don't know, but I will be paying attention, and so will Lulu.

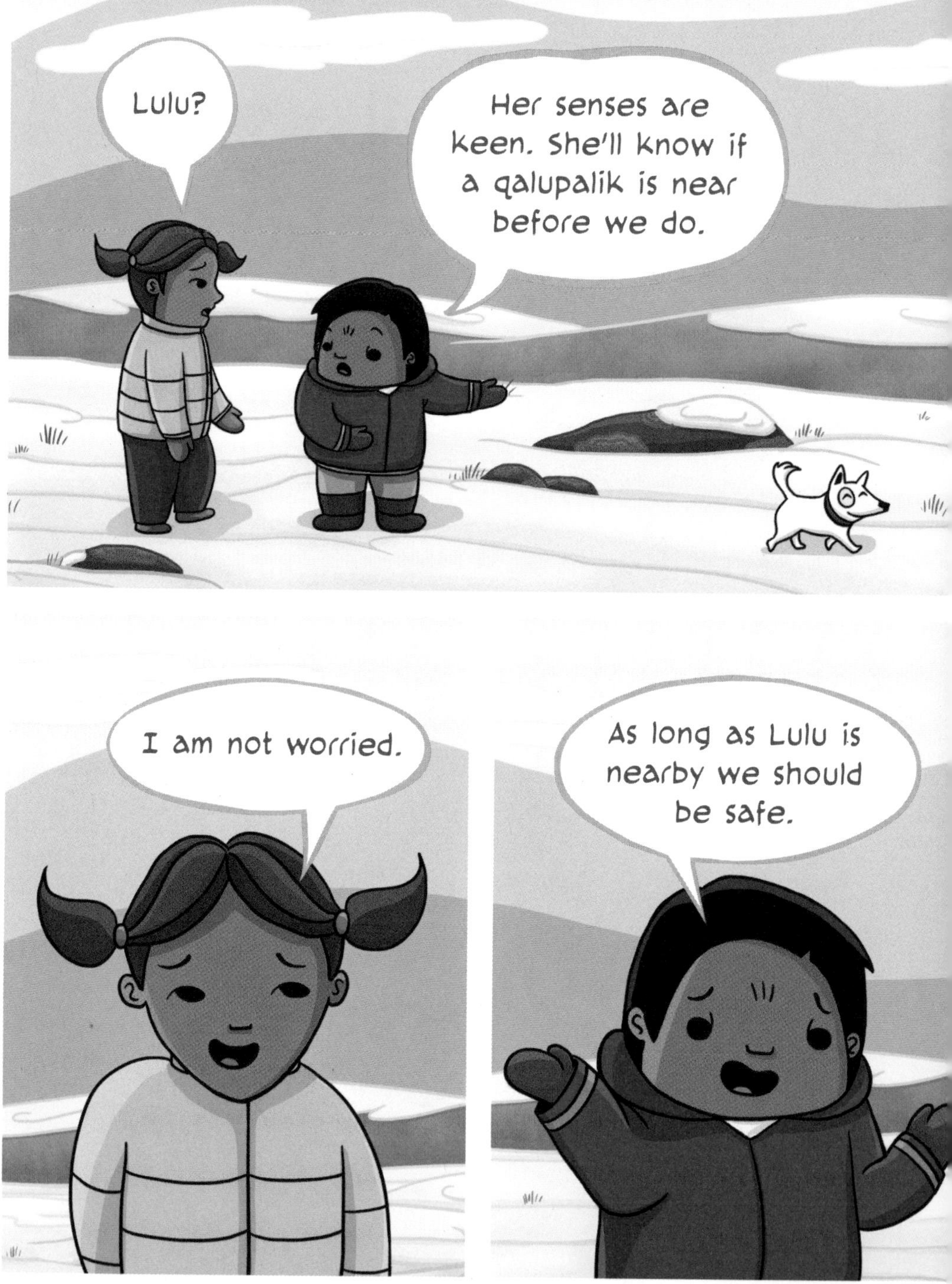
Lulu?
Her senses are keen. She'll know if a qalupalik is near before we do.
I am not worried.
As long as Lulu is nearby we should be safe.

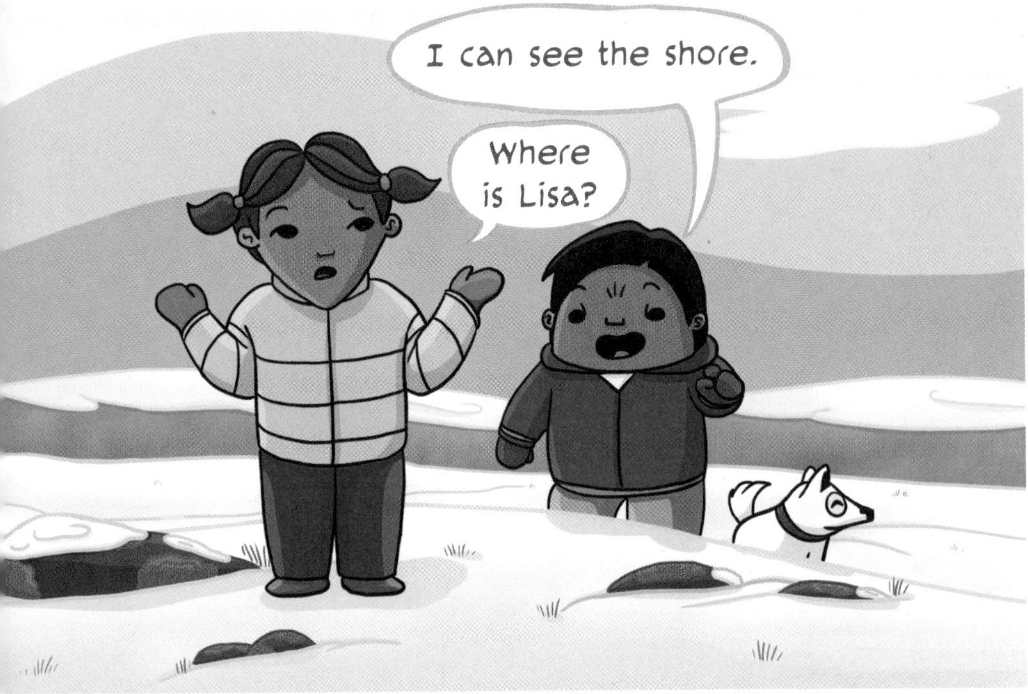
Where is Lisa?
I can see the shore.

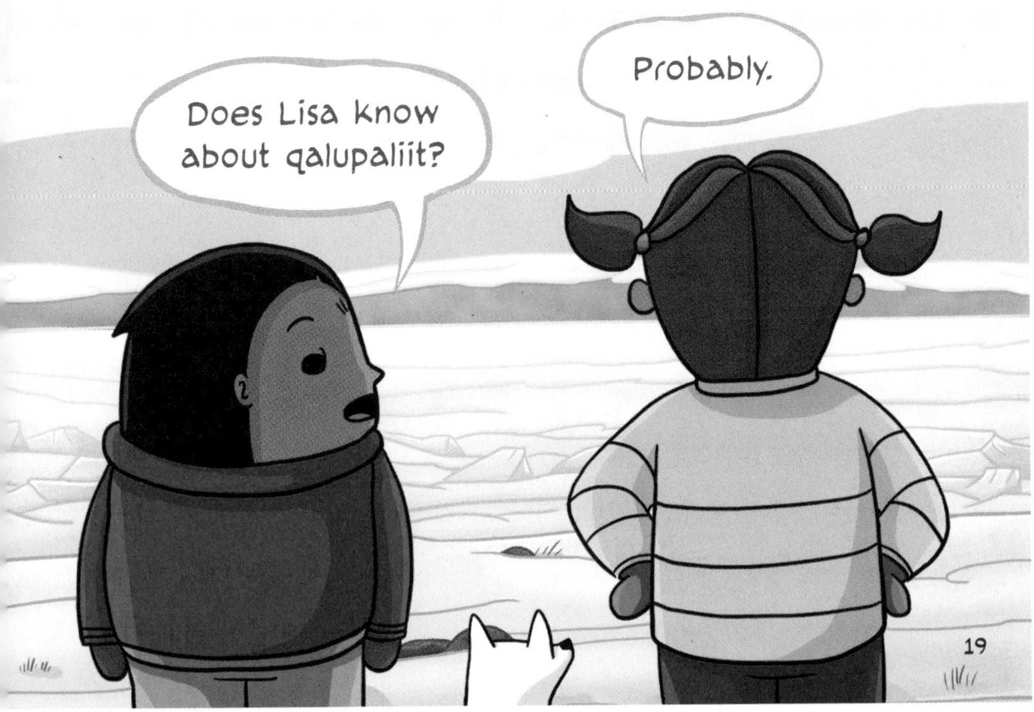
Does Lisa know about qalupaliit?
Probably.

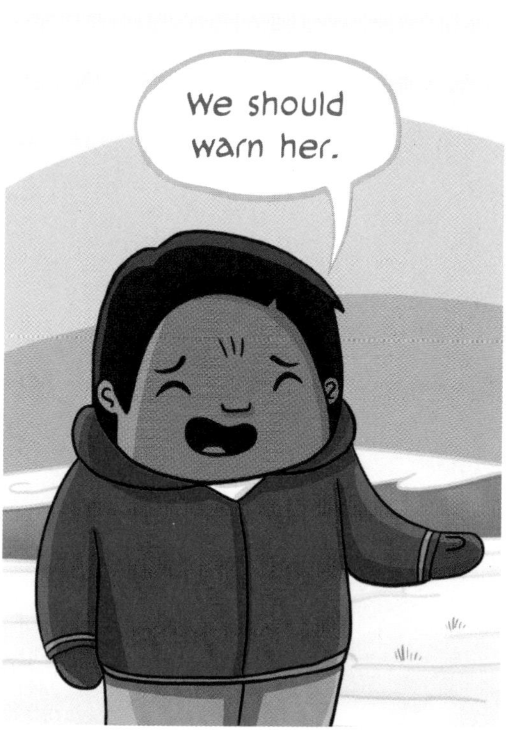
We should warn her.

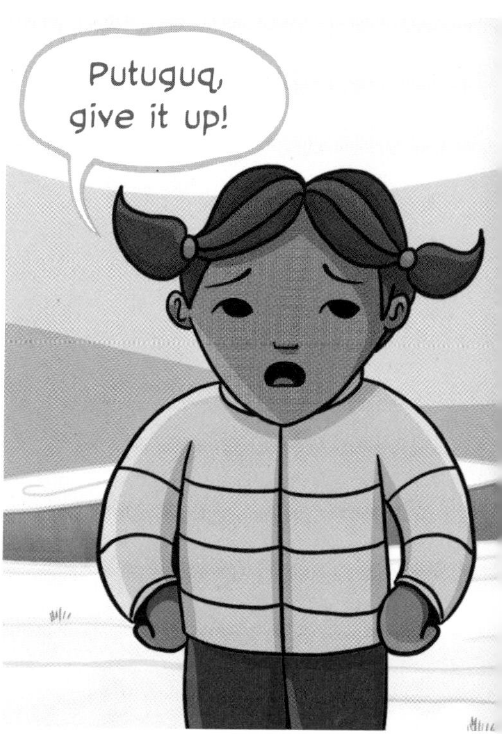
Putuguq, give it up!

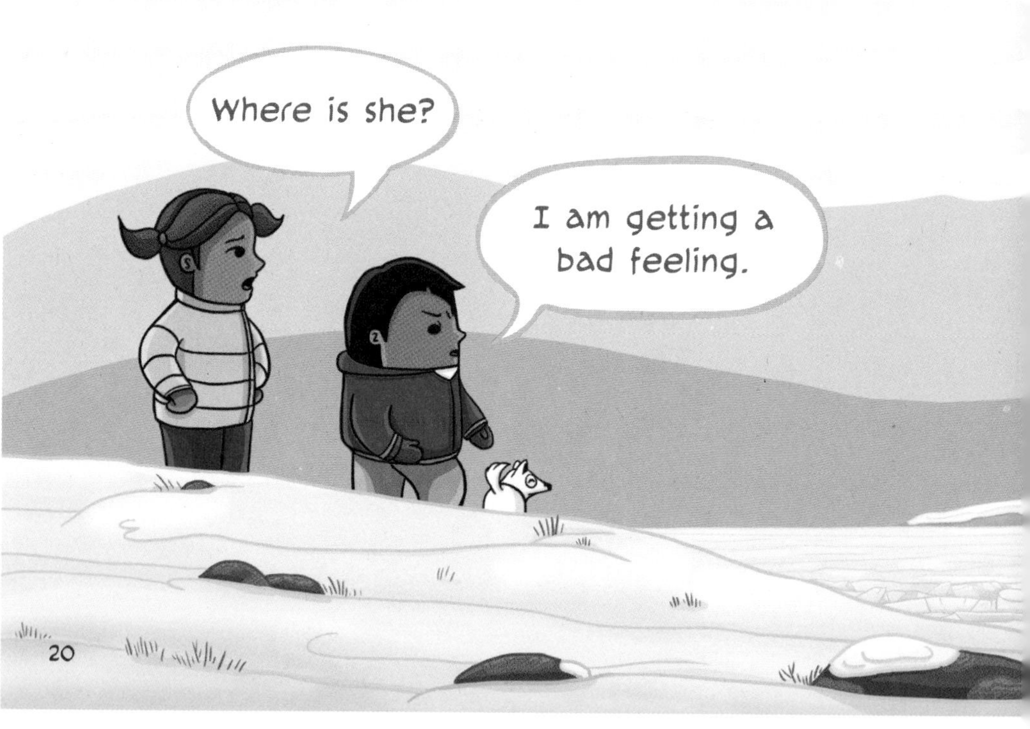
Where is she?
I am getting a bad feeling.

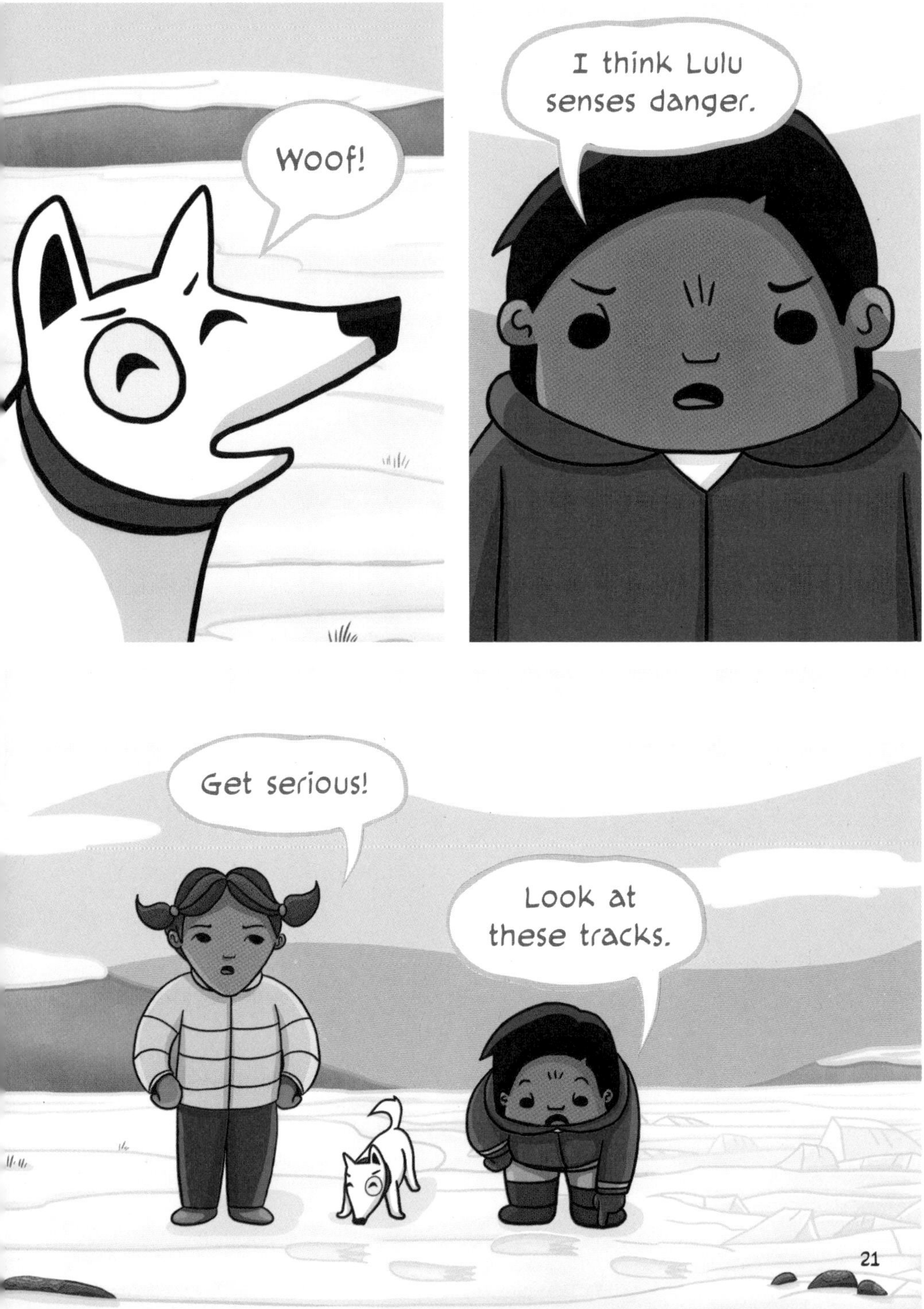
Woof!
I think Lulu senses danger.
Get serious!
Look at these tracks.

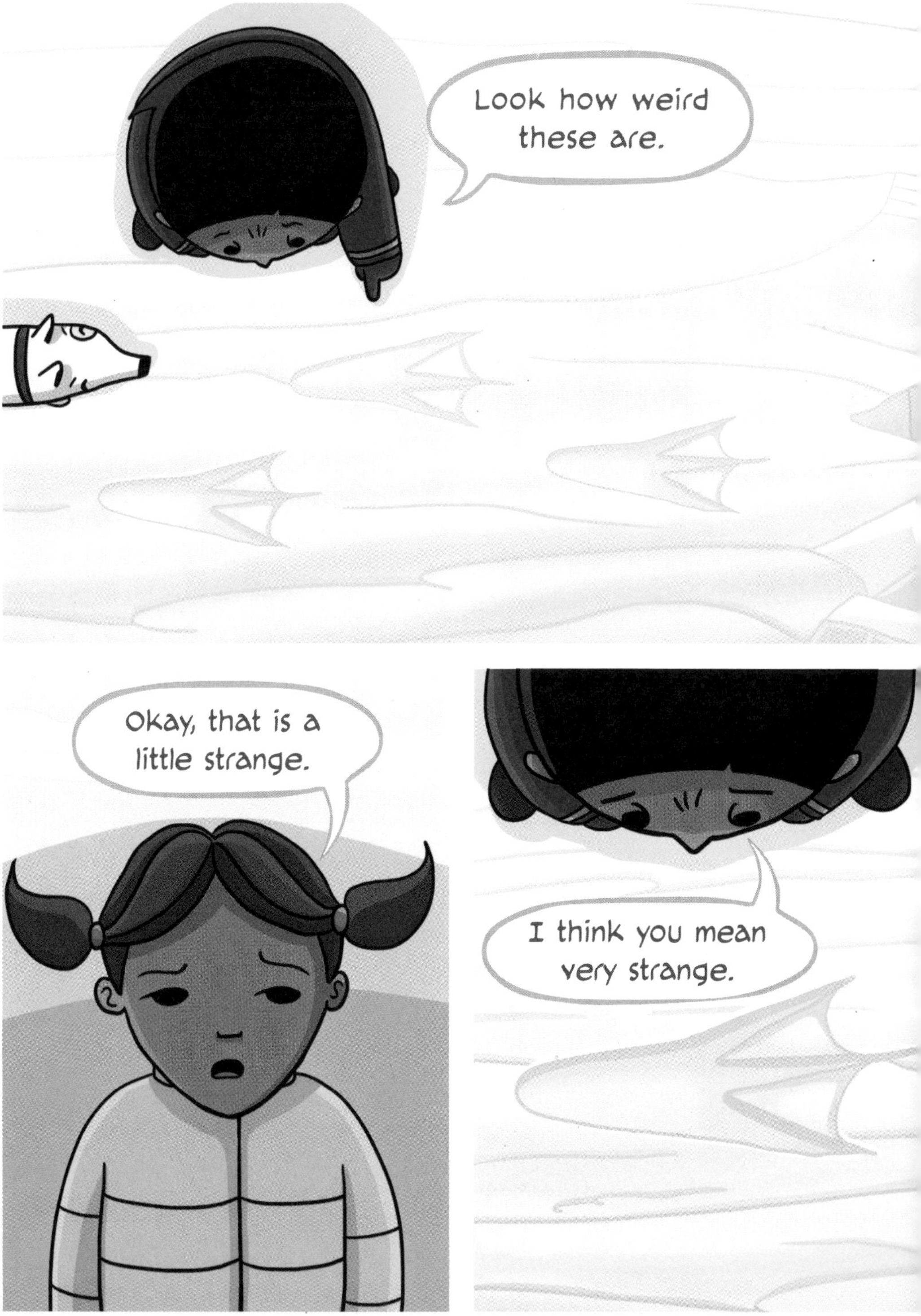
Look how weird these are.
Okay, that is a little strange.
I think you mean very strange.

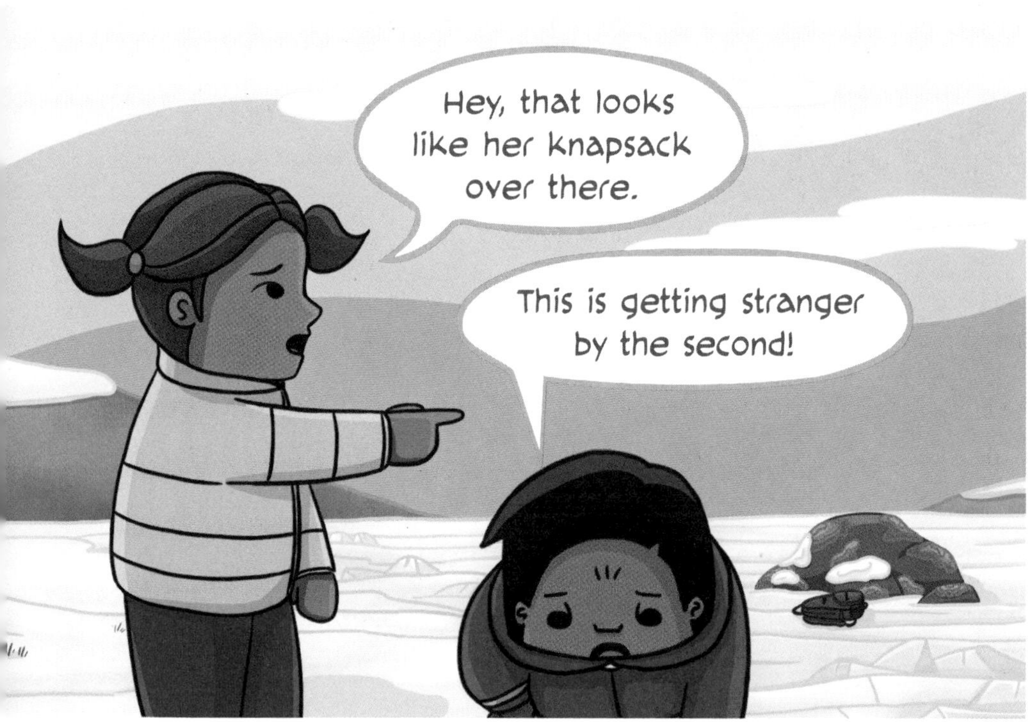
Hey, that looks like her knapsack over there.
This is getting stranger by the second!

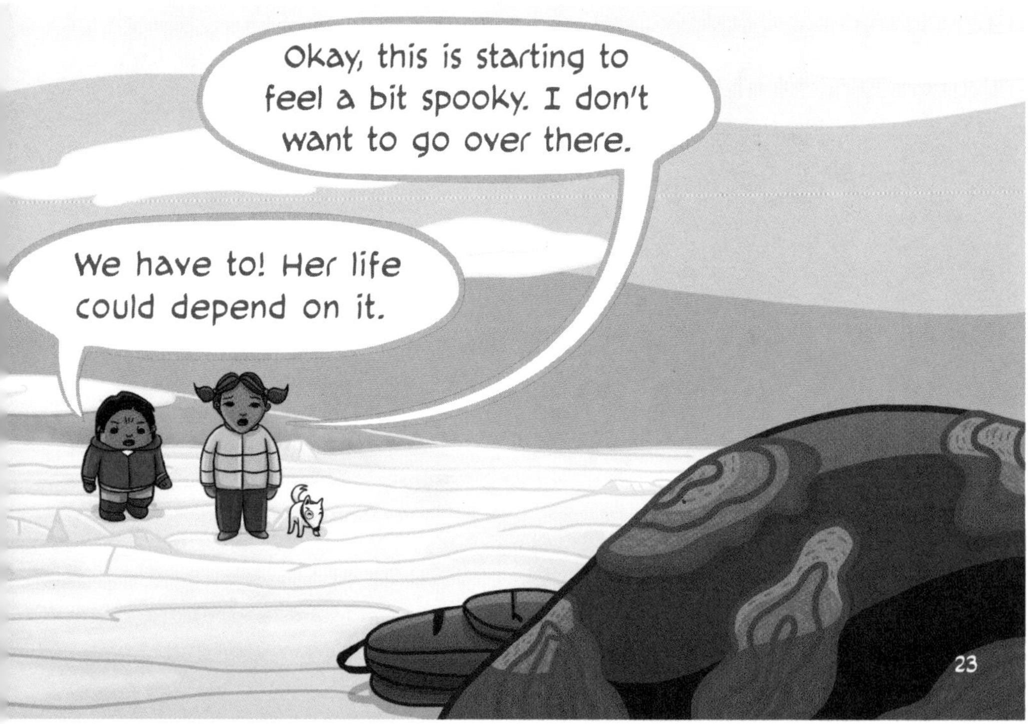
Okay, this is starting to feel a bit spooky. I don't want to go over there.
We have to! Her life could depend on it.

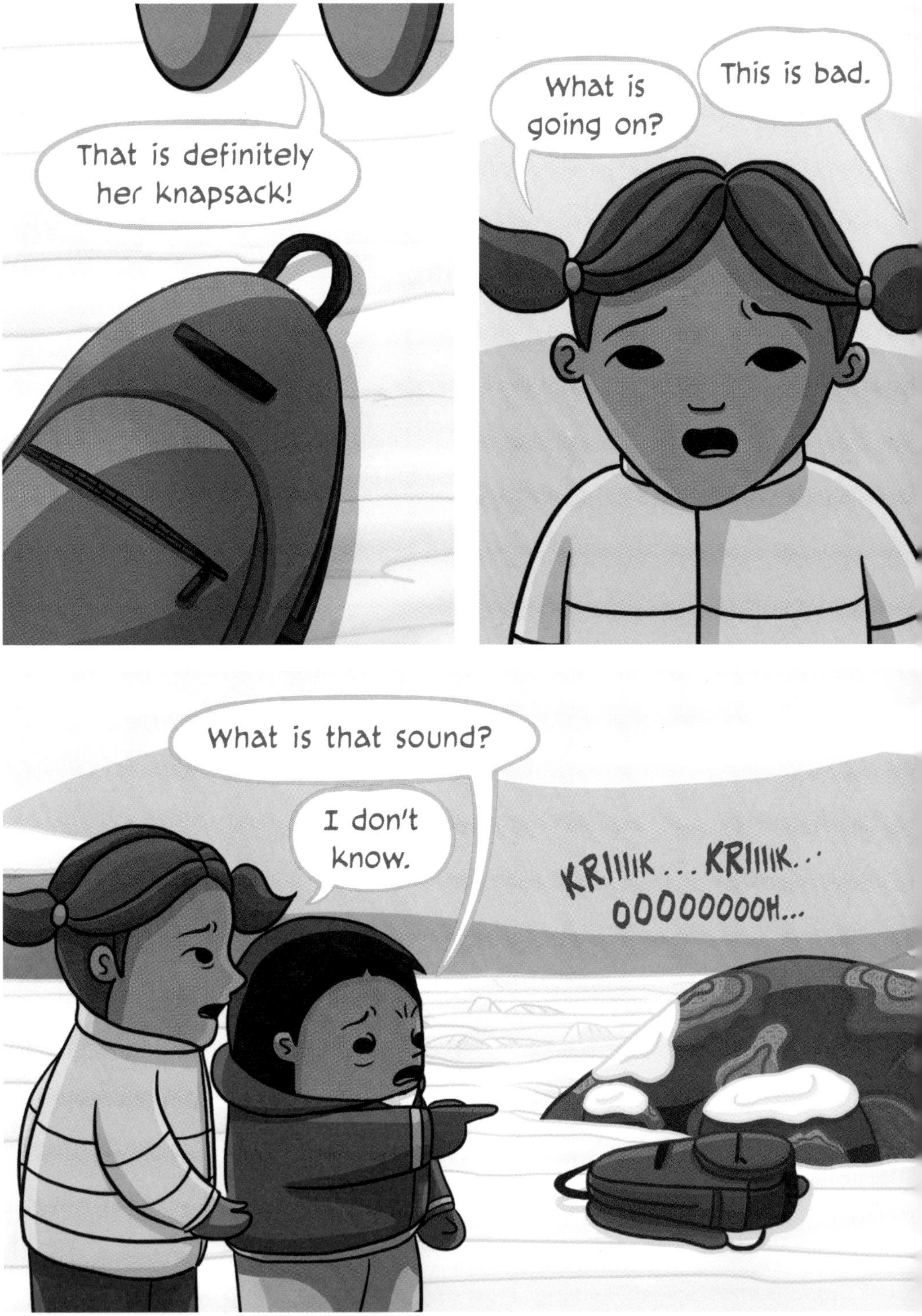
That is definitely her knapsack!
What is going on?
This is bad.
What is that sound?
I don't know.
KRIIIIK . . . KRIIIIK. . .
OOOOOOOOH...

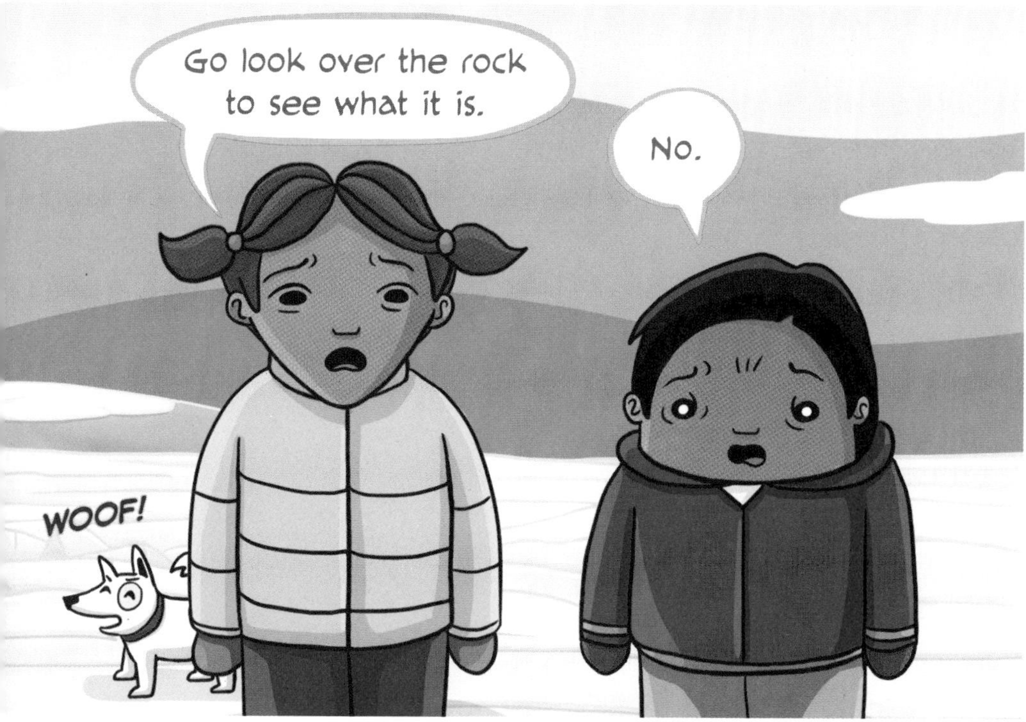
Go look over the rock to see what it is.
No.
WOOF!

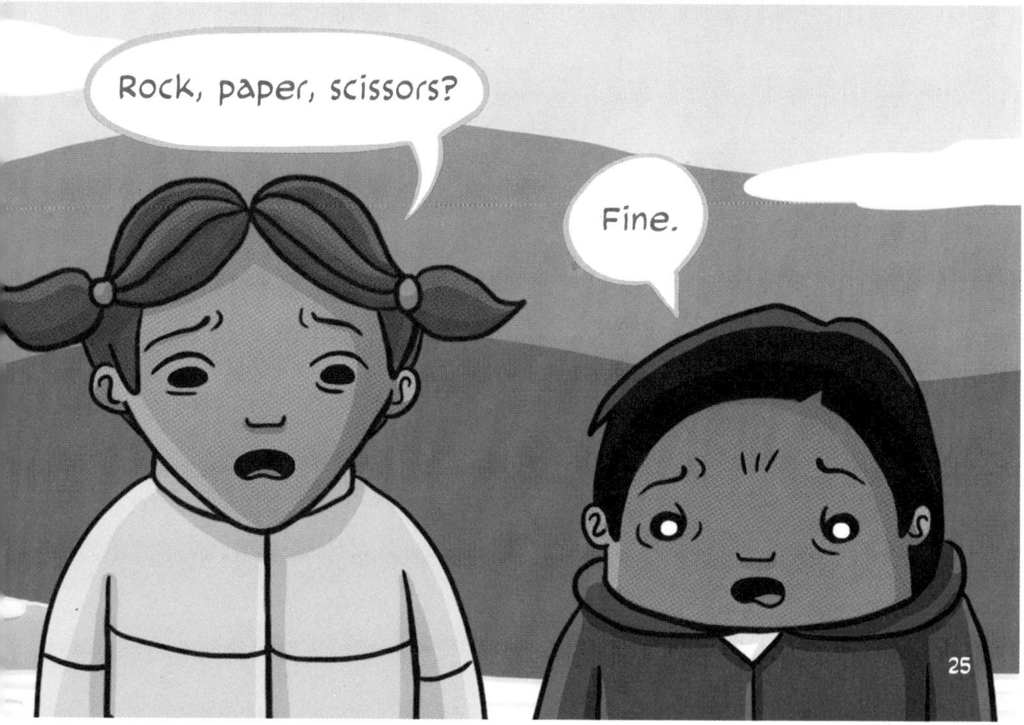
Rock, paper, scissors?
Fine.

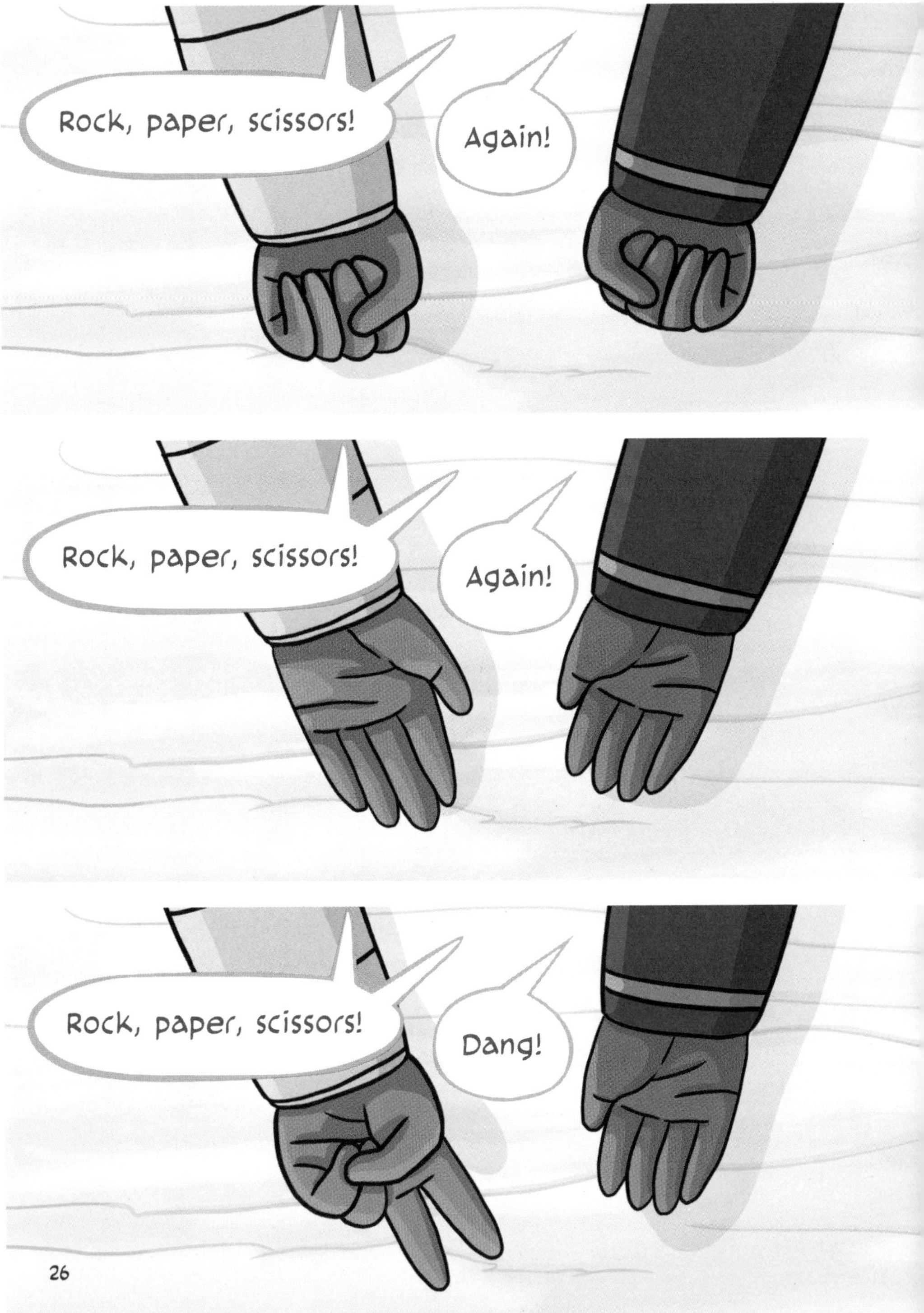
Rock, paper, scissors!
Again!
Rock, paper, scissors!
Again!
Rock, paper, scissors!
Dang!

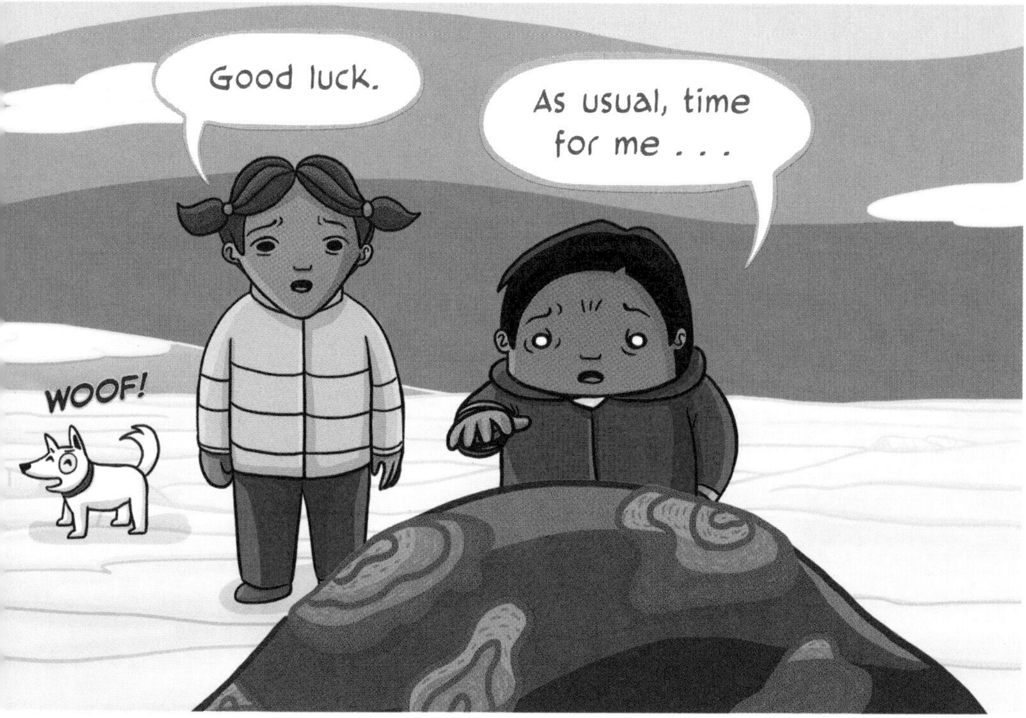
Good luck.
As usual, time for me . . .
WOOF!

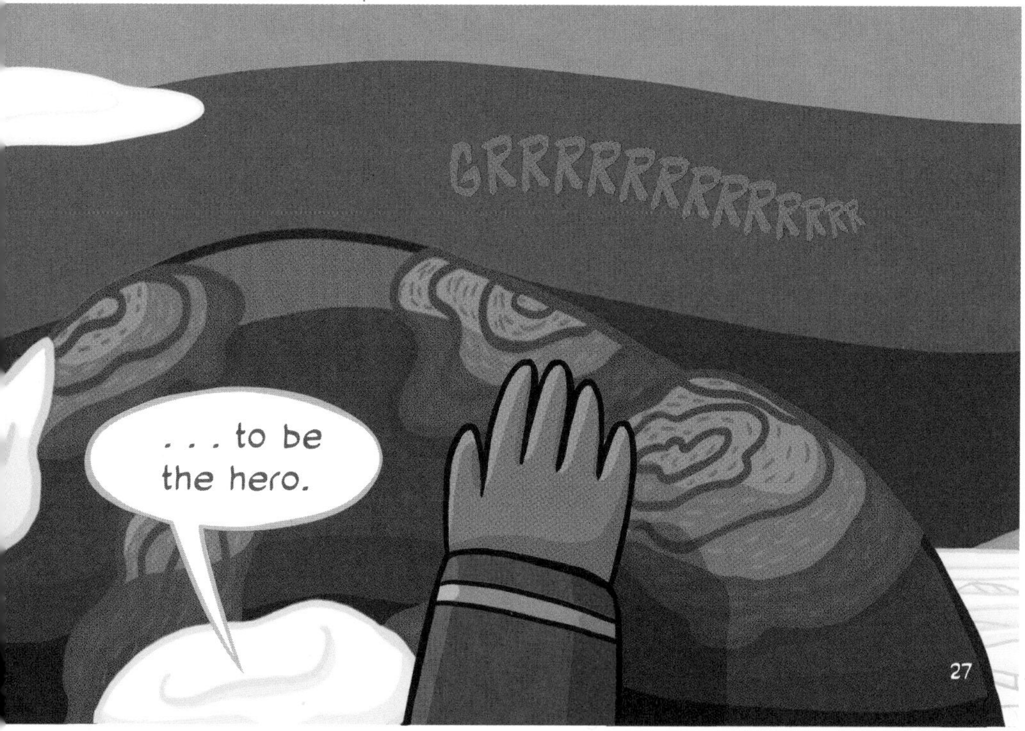
GRRRRRRRRRRRRR
. . . to be the hero.

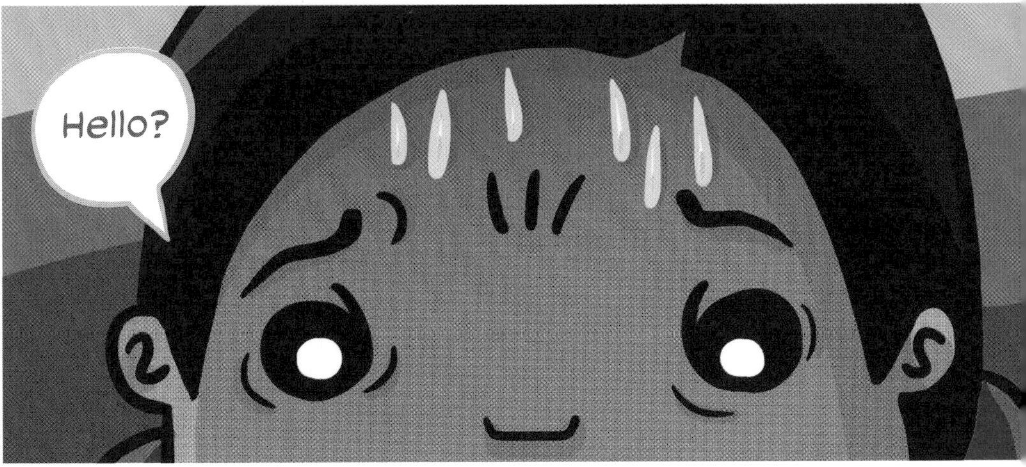
Hello?

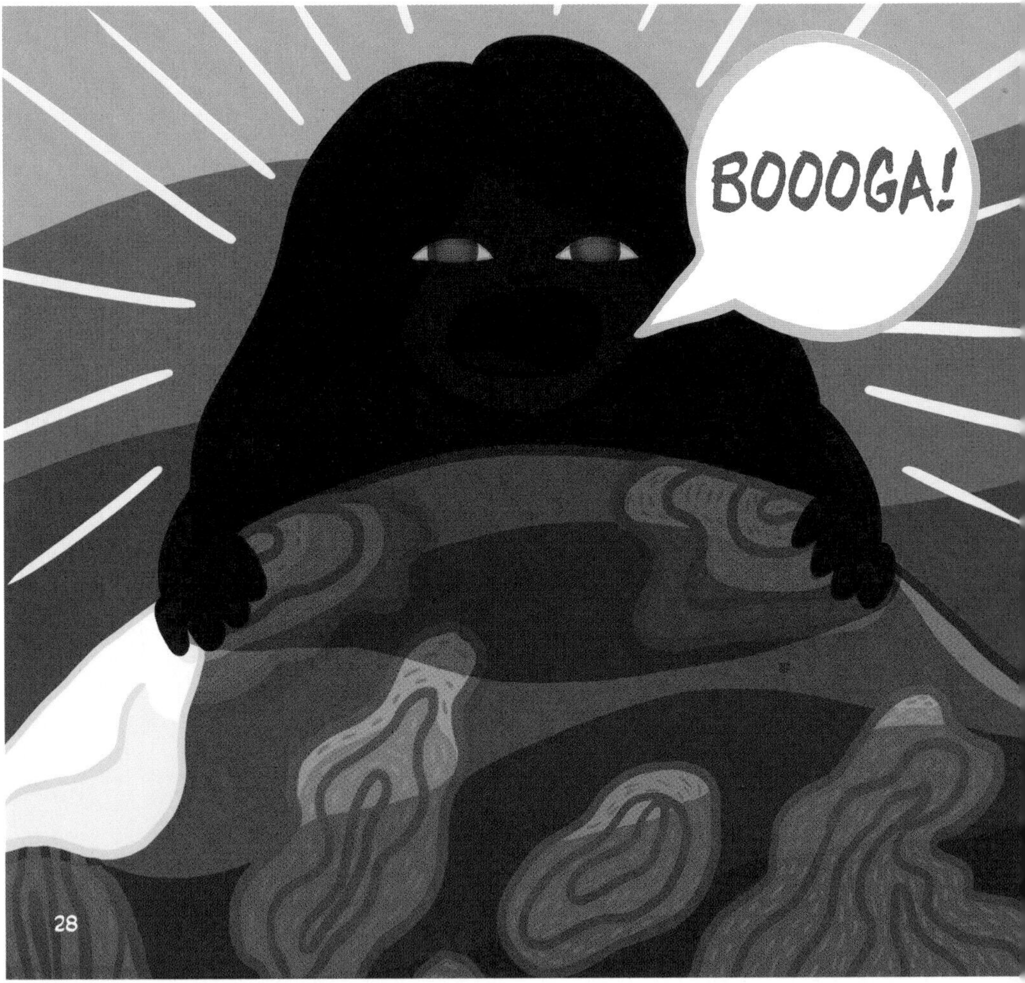
BOOOGA!

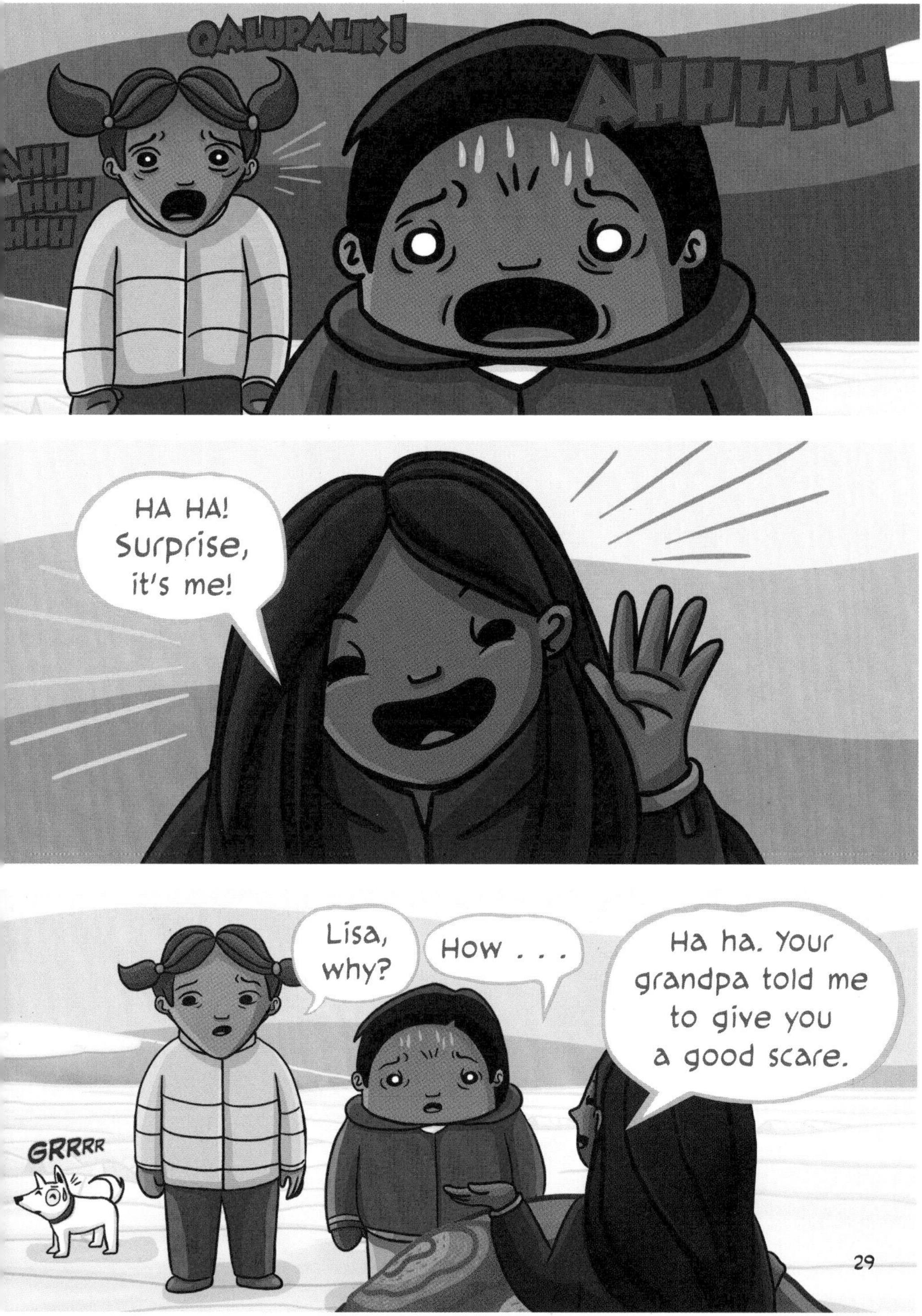

QALUPALIK!
AHHHHHH
HA HA! Surprise, it's me!
Lisa, why?
How . . .
Ha ha. Your grandpa told me to give you a good scare.
GRRRR

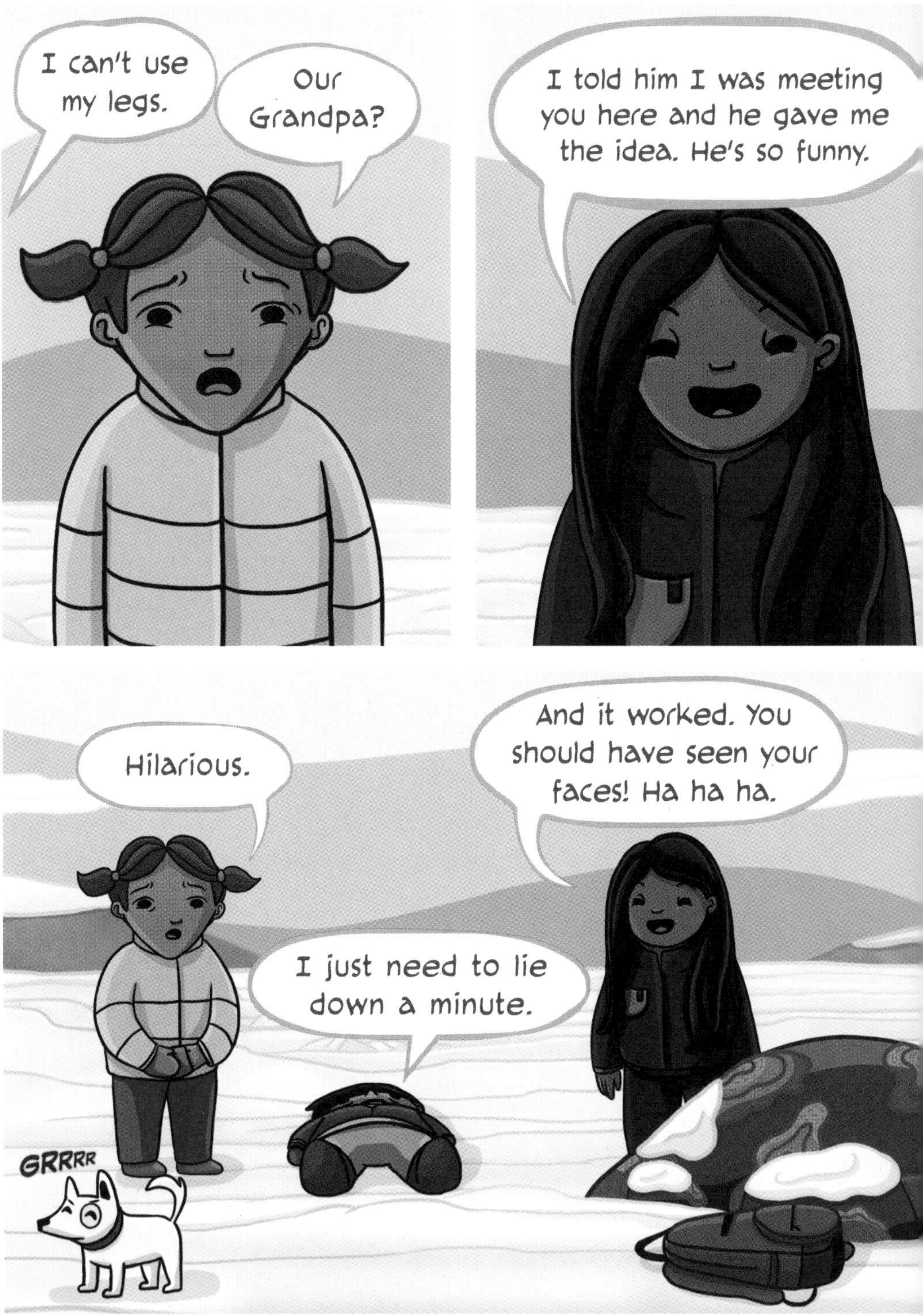
I can't use my legs.
Our Grandpa?
I told him I was meeting you here and he gave me the idea. He's so funny.
Hilarious.
And it worked. You should have seen your faces! Ha ha ha.
I just need to lie down a minute.
GRRRR

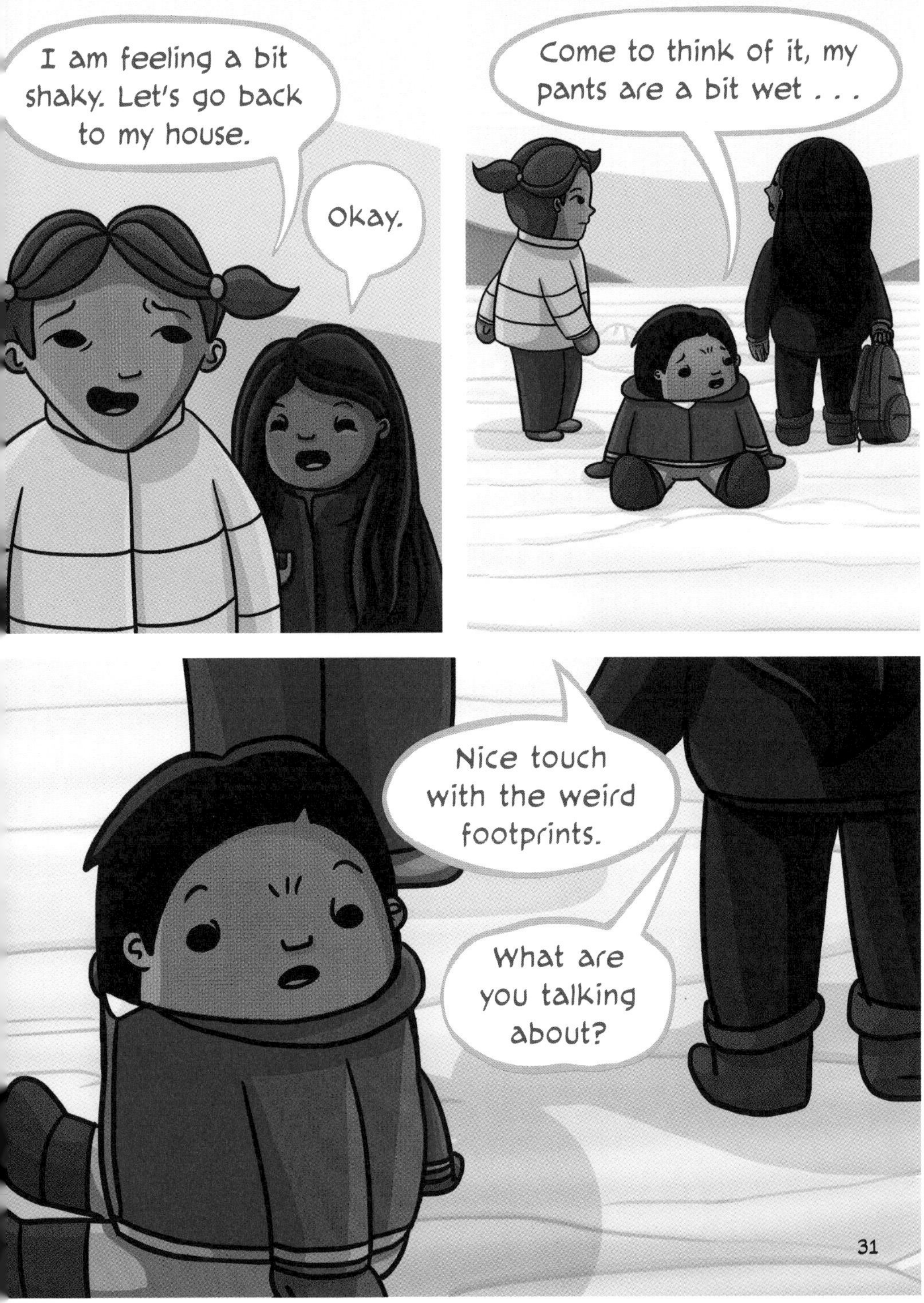
I am feeling a bit shaky. Let's go back to my house.
Okay.
Come to think of it, my pants are a bit wet . . .
Nice touch with the weird footprints.
What are you talking about?

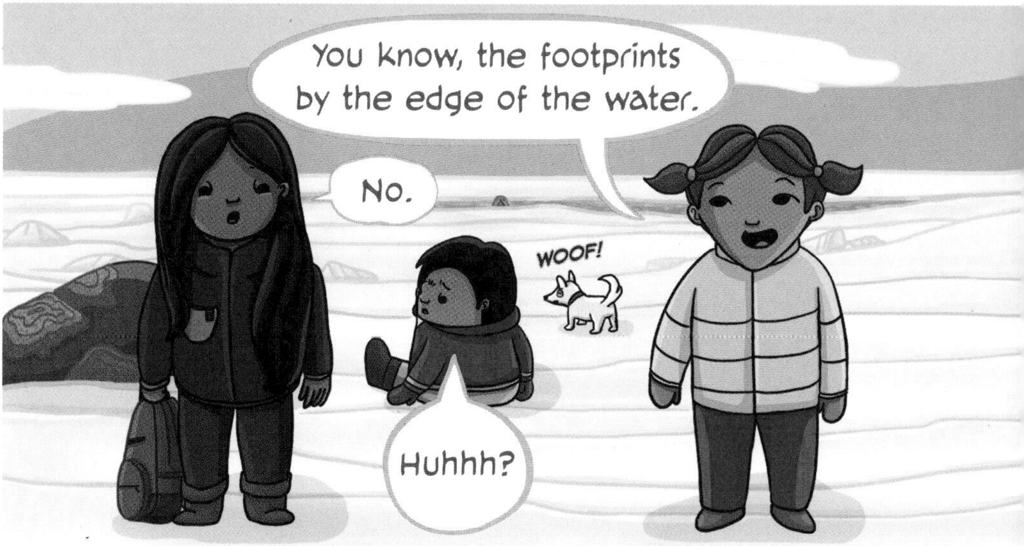
You know, the footprints by the edge of the water.
No.
WOOF!
Huhhh?

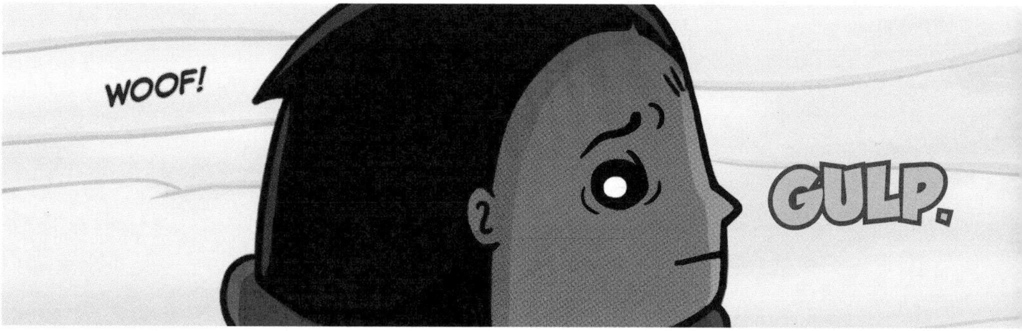
WOOF!
GULP.

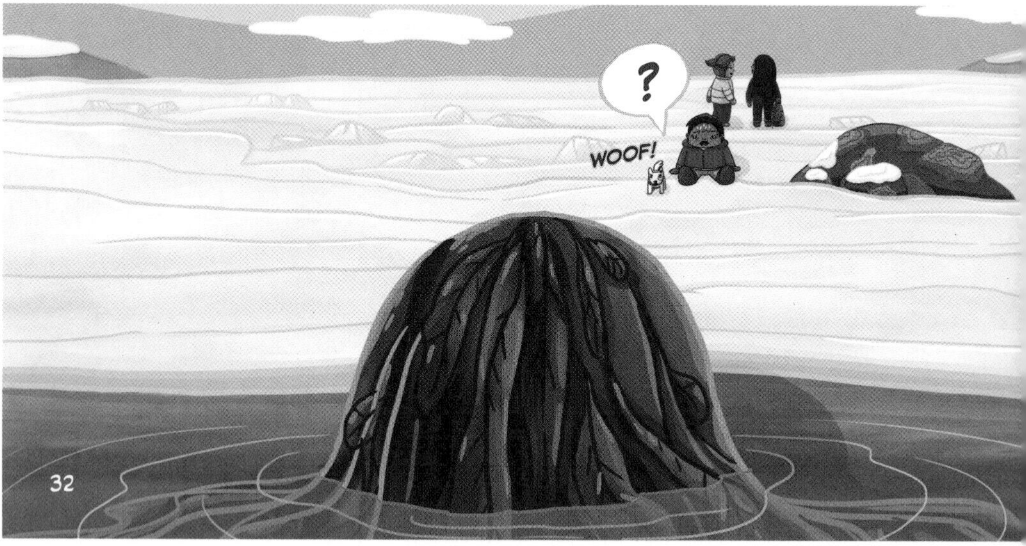
?
WOOF!

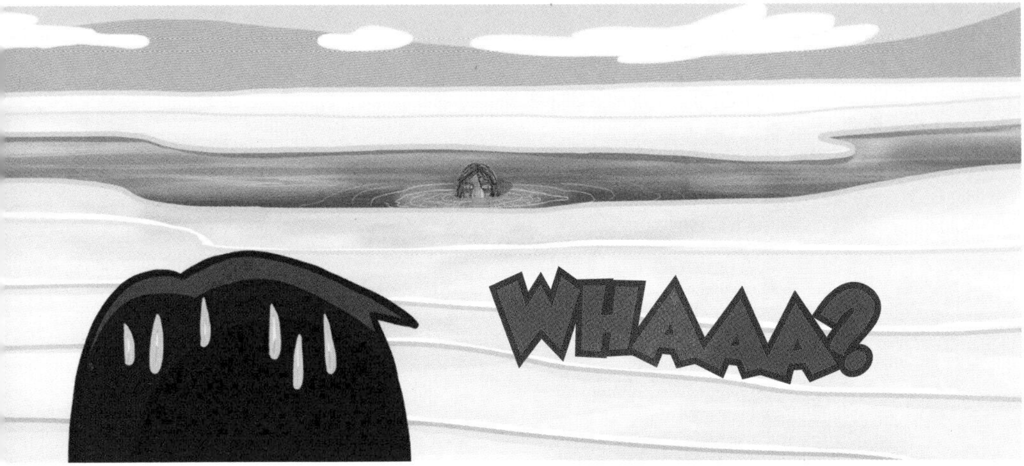
WHAAA?

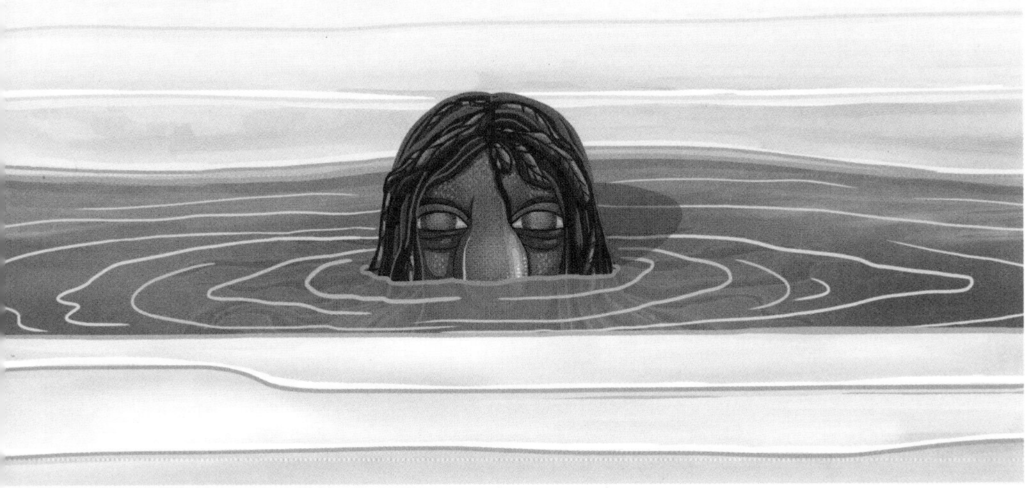

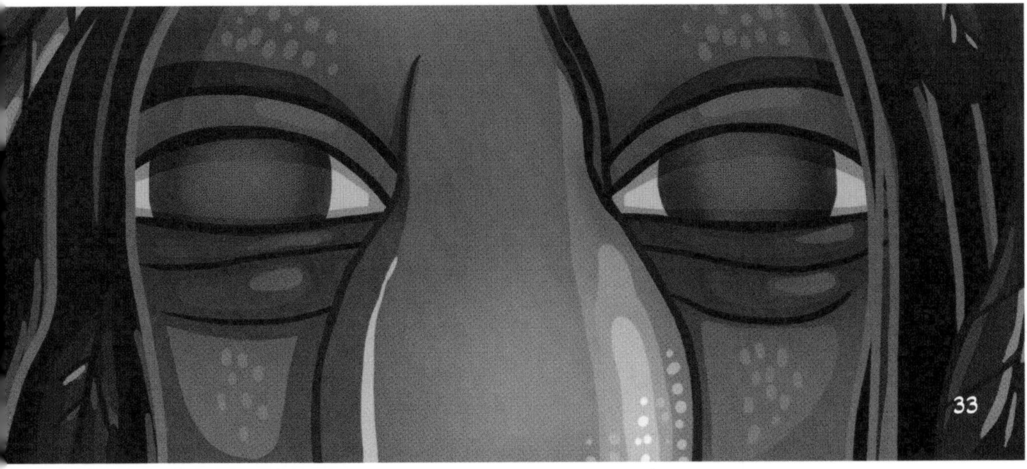

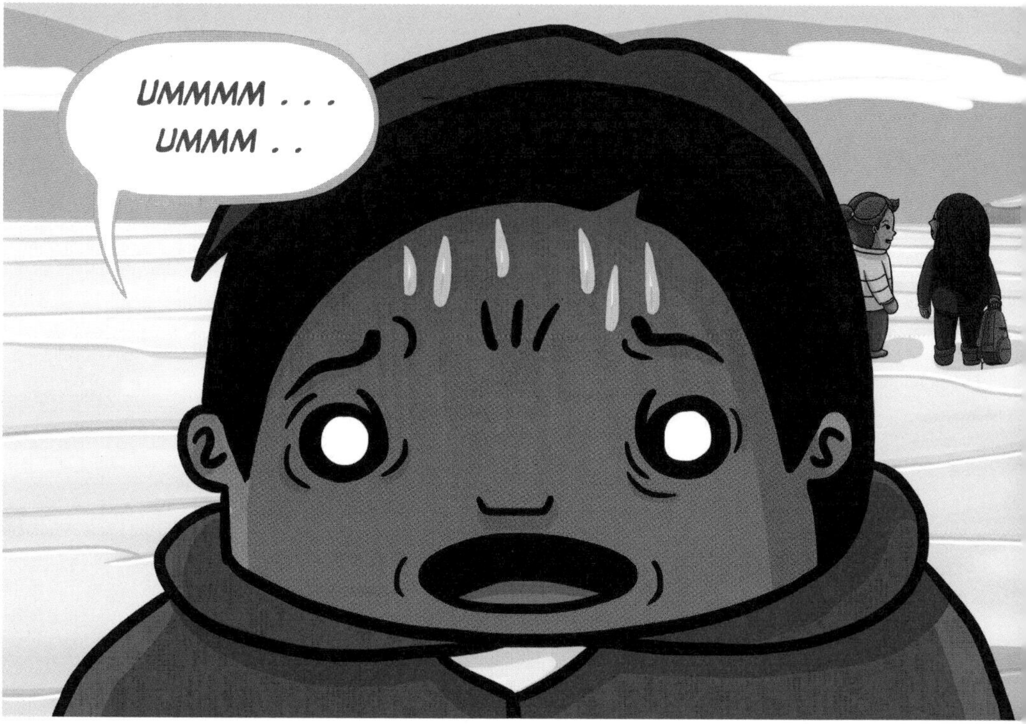
UMMMM . . .
UMMM . .

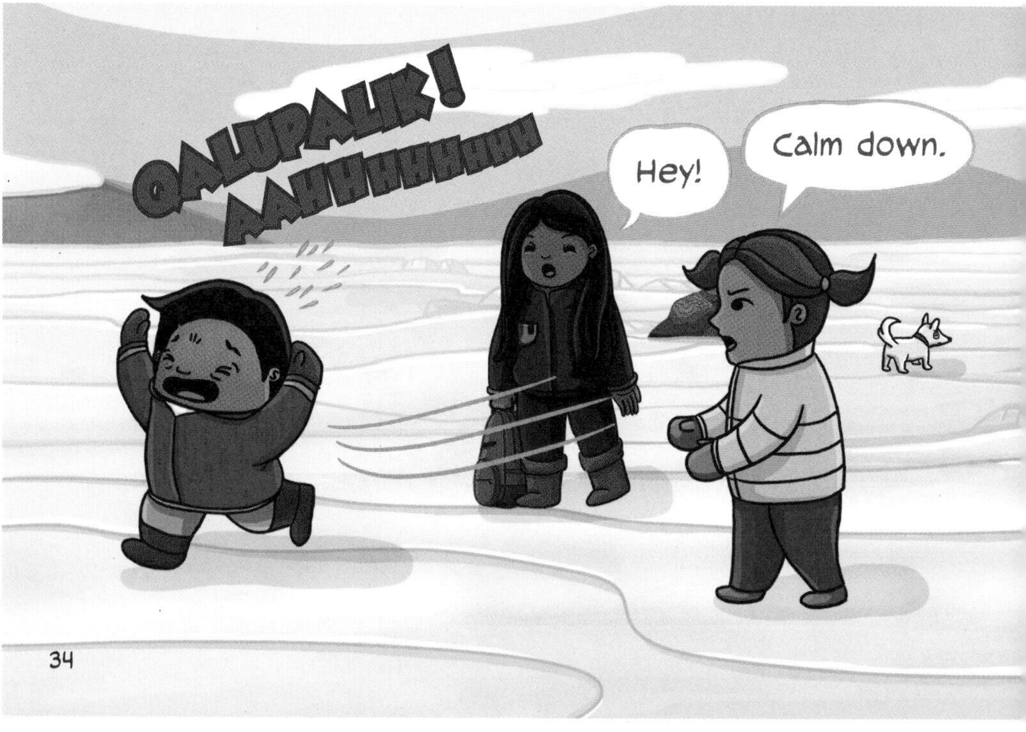
QALUPALIK!
AAHHHHHHHH
Hey!
Calm down.

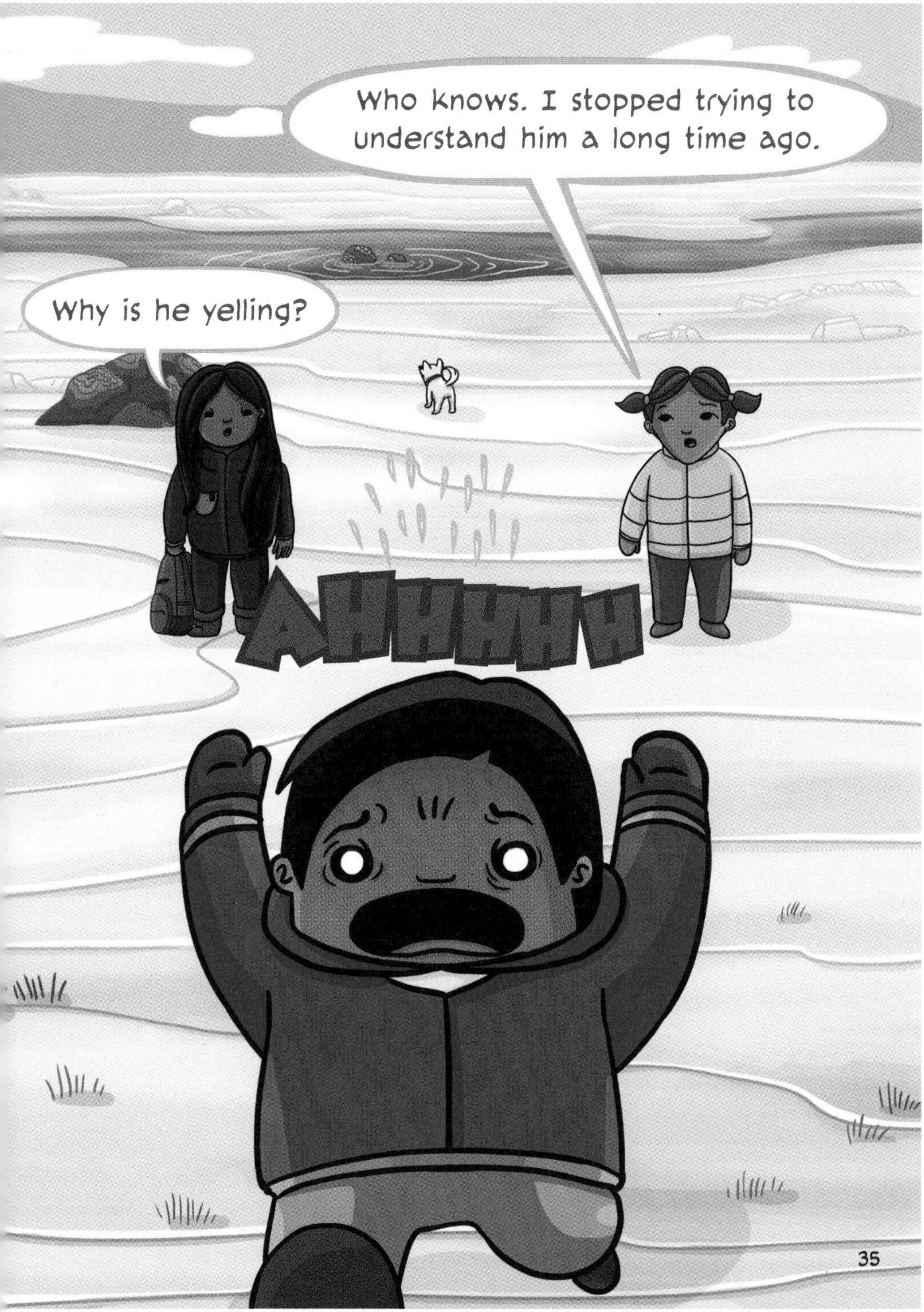
Why is he yelling?
Who knows. I stopped trying to understand him a long time ago.
AHHHHH

CONTRIBUTORS

Roselynn Akulukjuk was raised in Pangnirtung, Nunavut. In 2012, Roselynn moved to Toronto to pursue a career in film and attended the Toronto Film School, where she fell in love with being behind the camera. After her studies, Roselynn returned home to Nunavut, where she began working with Taqqut Productions, an Inuit-owned production company located in the capital of Nunavut, Iqaluit. Roselynn's short film *The Owl and the Lemming* was adapted for a children's book of the same name in 2016. The book has been nominated for the 2018 Blue Spruce Award and the 2017 Shining Willow Award and was included on the Cooperative Children's Book Centre's Best-of-2017 list.

Danny Christopher has travelled throughout the Canadian Arctic as an instructor for Nunavut Arctic College. He is the illustrator of *The Legend of the Fog*, *A Children's Guide to Arctic Birds*, and *Animals Illustrated: Polar Bear*. His work on *The Legend of the Fog* was nominated for the Amelia Frances Howard-Gibbon Illustration Award. He lives in Toronto with his wife, four children, and a little bulldog.

Astrid Arijanto is a designer and illustrator who spent her childhood drawing on any surface she could get her hands on, from papers to walls to all the white fences around her parents' house. Since then, her work has appeared in various media and publications across Canada and Asia. She lives in Toronto and spends most of her days designing and illustrating beautiful books.

QALUPALIIT

singular QALUPALIK

Qalupaliit (also spelled *qallupilluit*) are creatures that live in the sea. They have slimy, green skin like sculpin, and long hair and nails. They wear *amautiit* made of eider duck skin, and they use the amautiit to snatch children who wander along the shorelines of the Arctic. They are magical beings that can turn into any sea animal.

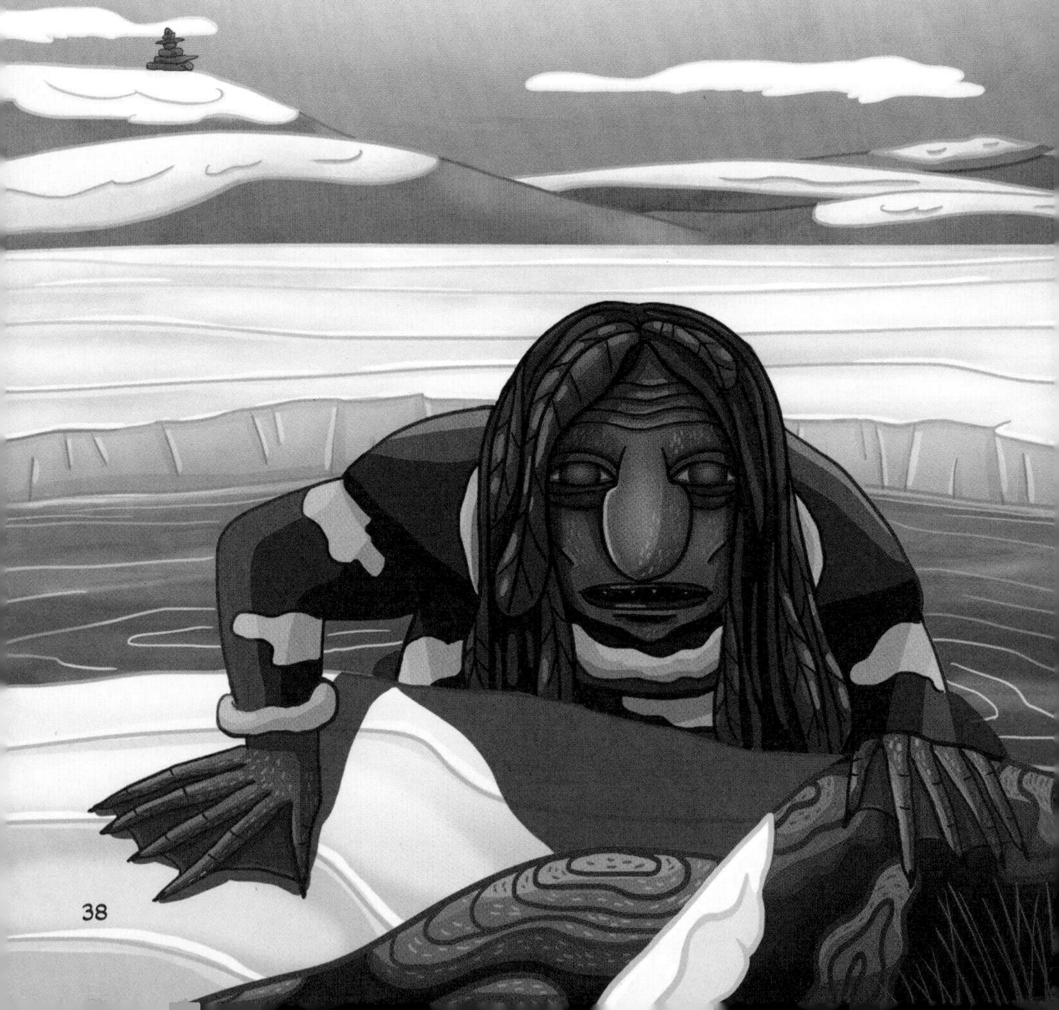

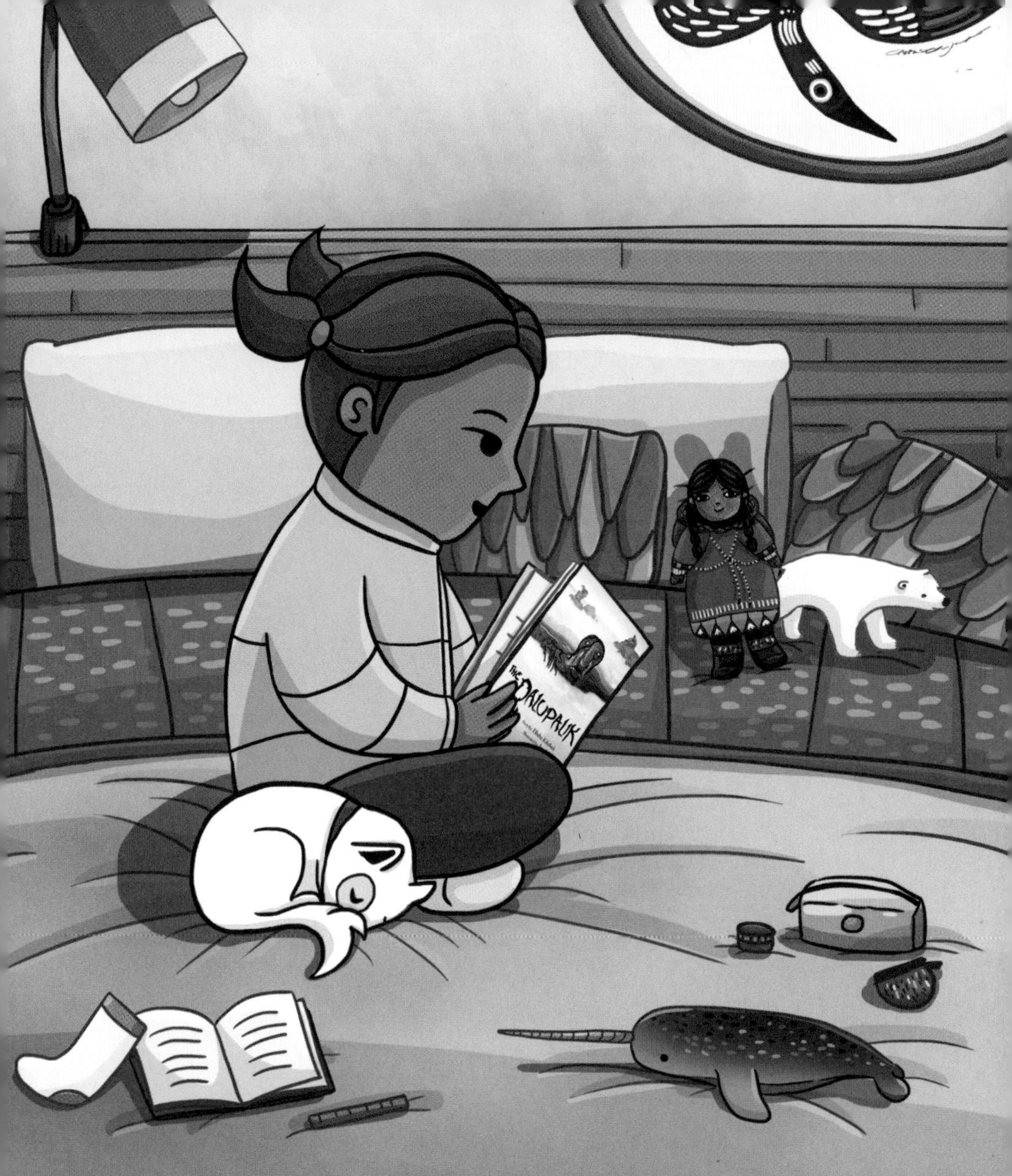
THE QALUPALIK

Want to learn more about qalupaliit?

Check out *The Qalupalik*, a book by Inuit storyteller Elisha Kilabuk. In it he shares a very old legend about how a little orphan once outsmarted a qalupalik!

DON'T MISS

the first Putuguq and Kublu adventure!

Putuguq & Kublu

By Danny Christopher • Illustrated by Astrid Arijanto

ISBN
978-1-77227-143-0
$5.95

INHABIT MEDIA

Iqaluit • Toronto